A PERVERSION OF JUSTICE

WHEN POWERFUL, DEPRAVED CRIMINALS
WILL GO TO ANY LENGTHS TO ESCAPE THE LAW

AUSTIN GREEN

Mereo Books

1A The Wool Market Dyer Street Cirencester Gloucestershire GL7 2PR
An imprint of Memoirs Books Ltd. www.mereobooks.com

A Perversion of Justice: 978-1-86151-927-6

First published in Great Britain in 2019
by Mereo Books, an imprint of Memoirs Books Ltd.

Copyright ©2019

Austin Green has asserted his right under the Copyright Designs and Patents
Act 1988 to be identified as the author of this work.

This book is a work of fiction and except in the case of historical fact any
resemblance to actual persons living or dead is purely coincidental.

A CIP catalogue record for this book is available from the British Library.
This book is sold subject to the condition that it shall not by way of trade
or otherwise be lent, resold, hired out or otherwise circulated without the
publisher's prior consent in any form of binding or cover, other than that in
which it is published and without a similar condition, including this condition
being imposed on the subsequent purchaser.

The address for Memoirs Books Ltd. can be
found at www.mereobooks.com

Memoirs Books Ltd. Reg. No. 7834348

Typeset in 11/15pt Century Schoolbook
by Wiltshire Associates Ltd.
Printed and bound in Great Britain by Biddles Books

"An event has happened upon which It is difficult to speak and impossible to be silent"

From a speech 5th May 1784 in the trial of Warren Hastings

Prologue

The main advance was already several hundred yards ahead as star shells lit up the pre-dawn sky.

"Must keep up…" The stretcher bearer's breathing was laboured, and every breath seemed to echo around his head. His feet were becoming bogged down in the wet mud, and he could feel his strength slowly ebbing away with each painful step. "Must get there, must help the men."

In the distance he could see his comrades diving for cover, hugging the muddy earth and desperately seeking refuge from the mortar shells that rained down upon them and the red tracers of bullets criss-crossing the terrain just above their heads. The screams of wounded soldiers stung his ears.

"Stretcher bearer… Must get there, the men…"

His legs finally gave way from under him and he crashed to his knees in the mud. The stretcher he was carrying fell from his grasp. He scrambled desperately to retrieve his hold, and as he did so the large brass cross fell from around his neck and dangled in front of him. He gripped it with mud-covered hands.

"Please god, help me!"

As he pleaded with his god, the figure of an enemy soldier rushed at him from out of the mist, his rifle held high with its bayonet glinting its deadly intention. The stretcher bearer fell backwards into the mud, his body gripped by fear as he tried to scramble away. As he did so his brass cross bounced from side to side upon his chest, and just for a brief moment he could see his foe clearly.

"Dear god, he's just a boy!" he muttered.

His strength finally exhausted, he lay on his back in the mud accepting his fate. He looked into the boy soldier's face and for a moment they seemed to be locked in time. It was such a young face. The boy appeared to be no more than sixteen.

Closer, closer, closer, the boy soldier advanced. In a desperate attempt at survival, the stretcher bearer ripped open his battledress to reveal his clerical collar. The young soldier stopped as though mesmerised by the sight of this holy man laying helpless in the mud.

"Pardon padre, pardon, pardon!" he said. He dropped

his rifle in the mud and began to weep. Then he turned and ran.

"Not that way!" shouted the stretcher bearer. But no sooner had he shouted his warning than a mine exploded under the fleeing soldier and tossed him into the air like a feather pillow. His limp and twisted body crashed into the mud a few yards away. The holy man crawled towards the bloody remains, cradled the head of the boy soldier and looked up to heavens. "Why?" he screamed.

Daniel Carter awoke from his nightmare, his body drenched in sweat in the early morning light. He looked at his hands, half expecting them to be covered in the boy soldier's blood, but there was none. He glanced around the room to reassure himself that it had just been a bad dream, but it was more than a bad dream; it was another of the reminders of his army life that kept invading his sleep. His dreams were often troubled, and when they were they always involved blood, war and conflict.

Chapter 1

The Reverend Daniel Leo Carter, or 'Dan the man', as he was affectionately known by the younger parishioners in the village of Etwell, quietly closed the door of his cottage behind him, hunched his shoulders against the crisp morning air and surveyed his small garden. His housekeeper, Mrs Schneider, had passed away only a few days earlier after a mercifully short illness, but already it seemed that its once neatly-trimmed borders and formerly weedless flowerbeds were beginning to show signs of her absence.

Ethel Schneider loved pottering in the Reverend Carter's garden. In fact there wasn't much that she didn't love doing for him. From the moment he had first arrived at St Andrew's after his unexpected but none the less welcome elevation from army chaplain to parish priest, she had more or less taken over. She had done everything for him, and now she was gone. Ethel had been more than just Daniel's housekeeper; she had been a friend. She had lifted his spirits when he was down. He had no family of his own after his parents had been killed in a car crash and she had become, perhaps unconsciously, his mother and grandmother rolled into one.

"What am I going to do without you?" Daniel murmured to himself.

In one corner of the driveway stood his beloved old Hillman Minx. Its battered and rusted body showed every one of its forty years, but it still got him from A to B and as most of his journeys were around the village, when it did break down, which was often, there was always someone on hand to help him get it started or tow him home, and this was quite a common sight in the village. In fact he often thought his old car was better recognised than he was.

He opened the boot, pulled out a sweater and put it on.

"I suppose I should get someone in to sort you out as well," he said, patting the car's roof like a man patting his pet dog. He closed the boot and began walking up the long gravel driveway that led to the lane, the memory of his nightmare fading as he did so.

The driveway divided two properties which were much larger and grander than his little cottage, particularly one of them. The house on his right was an imposing building with several bedrooms, surrounded by a large, well-manicured lawn. The Jacksons, who owned the property, hosted regular charitable and fundraising events for the church in their garden, of the kind that are an important part of the life of any village.

Daniel got on very well with Ken Jackson, as he too was an ex-Para. Added to the fact that Ken was an avid home brew man, this meant that they spent many evenings reliving old exploits, as only people who have served in the forces can. Their stories generally became more and more exaggerated as the effects of Ken's home brew took hold. They had been such great evenings, thought Daniel. They would have to do that again soon.

The other side of the driveway was a stark contrast. The once magnificent Edwardian façade of the old vicarage was now a burnt-out shell, engulfed by the advance of Mother Nature. The three chimneys that had once stood tall and proud had long since crashed into the centre of the house, and a few charred beams were all that remained of the roof. Even part of the exterior wall had collapsed, exposing what was left of the heart of the house.

The undergrowth was so dense that from the lane at the front of the house, a visitor to the village passing by would be unaware that only a few yards from where they stood lay the remains of the old vicarage of St Andrew's. Only a rusting sign saying 'DANGEROUS STRUCTURE – KEEP OUT" gave any clue that a building stood there at all.

Daniel stood and looked at the burnt-out shell which in an earlier time would have been his home. "What a waste," he said quietly to himself.

The fire that had destroyed this once proud and historic house had also claimed the life of his predecessor. The Reverend Joseph Winterbourne had been the Vicar at St. Andrew's for a number of years and by all accounts had been well respected, not just by his parishioners but by all the people of Etwell. William Schneider, husband of Ethel, or Bill as he was known locally had also perished in the fire in a vain attempt to save the Reverend Winterbourne. He was employed as the gravedigger, general handyman and gardener and by all accounts was very good at his work. He too had been a respected member of the community. Both men were buried in the church cemetery, which was less than a stone's throw from where they had died, just the other side of the lane, in fact right opposite the old vicarage where they had met their end.

What made this day perhaps even more poignant, especially for those who knew Ethel, was that this morning she was to be buried alongside her beloved husband Bill.

It was still only 6 am, but Daniel wanted Ethel's funeral to run smoothly. Not that Ethel would have wanted any fuss made over her, but Daniel knew that most of the village would be there to pay their respects and he wanted things to be right for them and for his old friend.

Ethel and Bill had been very popular in the village and were always willing to lend a hand. Indeed, when Daniel had been offered the position of Vicar of St. Andrew's, it was Ethel who was the first to greet him. The transition from army chaplain to village vicar had not been an easy one, but Ethel had always been there to offer advice and smooth his path, something for which Daniel was forever grateful.

Everything had been very strange at first, but that was three years ago and although it had taken some time for the villagers to get used to him and his laid-back manner, he felt that he was now accepted by his parishioners, and perhaps more importantly, he felt he belonged.

It had been difficult, to say the least. Daniel was not your average vicar. To start with he very rarely wore his clerical collar. Jeans and T-shirt were more his style, and the way he drove around the village in his beaten-up old car and regular visits to his local pub, Ye Olde Kings Head, had driven some of his flock to write to the Bishop. Ethel had told him several times that he was just rebelling from years of enforced army discipline, and of course she was right. She usually was.

He knew that the service this morning would be well attended, and not just by villagers. Several dignitaries were expected. Even the Reverend Winterbourne's brother, a prominent politician, had written to say he was coming. The village school had been given permission to close for the morning, so that pupils and staff could attend.

Oh yes, Ethel had been popular all right, thought Daniel. All the more reason to get it right.

He continued along the driveway towards the lane and swung back the large wooden gate that marked its entrance. He glanced again at the burnt-out shell of the vicarage. There had been much speculation and gossip in the village surrounding the demise of the two popular men. It had obviously been a very intense fire, you only had to look at the building to see that, but everyone seemed to have a different theory on how it had started. Many of these theories were expounded over a pint at Tommy's, as the Olde Kings Head was known to the locals, and were usually forgotten by the following day.

Daniel's thoughts returned to the Schneiders. Even though he'd had plenty of time, he had still not decided what to say at the service. They had obviously been a very loving couple. Daniel recalled how Mrs Schneider was always regaling him with tales about her late husband; how handsome he was, how romantic, how she missed cuddling up to him. This was usually just before she started on him about his lifestyle and how untidy he was and how he should find himself a good woman to look after him.

"Everyone should have someone to cuddle," she would say. "Why don't you find yourself a girlfriend? You're not bad looking for a vicar." A girlfriend! He chuckled to himself. Chance would be a fine thing.

Being a village vicar was not all tea parties and jumble sales. Daniel had just finished the busiest weekend of the year. Two services on Good Friday, two weddings on Saturday, then the Easter Sunday service, followed by the village fete on Bank Holiday Monday, and now he was up bright and early preparing to lay his old friend to rest.

Bill and Ethel had arrived in the country just before the outbreak of the Second World War and ended up settling in Etwell. They were obviously highly thought of, because at a time when German nationals were either being interned or repatriated, the people of the village rallied around to prevent the authorities from doing this with Bill and Ethel. Many of Daniel's older parishioners liked to recall how when the authorities came asking questions, they simply moved them to another house. Rumour had it that they even stayed in the village police house at one point. Either the authorities gave up the chase, or someone with common sense decided that the Schneiders were no threat to national security.

Daniel closed the gate behind him and stepped out into the lane that separated his home from the cemetery opposite. He looked to his right, up the lane towards his church. Its imposing façade stood proud against the dawn sky. The cemetery where Ethel would later be laid to rest stretched out with military precision towards him. Its neat hedges and borders and elegant flint wall were in stark contrast to the old churchyard that lay at the other end of the lane to his left. Only the tower remained of the fifteenth-century church. Its four turreted corners seemed to struggle over the trees and undergrowth as if gasping for breath, unlike the old vicarage, which had long since given up the battle.

The old church had been knocked down in the 1800s and a new church built to accommodate the increase in population. After years of neglect the graveyard had become very overgrown, and several of the headstones had fallen into disrepair or had even sunk beneath the ground entirely. The family and friends of those interred were either dead themselves or had moved away, but whenever Daniel had time he liked to take the long way to his church past the old church tower, and this was such a morning. It was so peaceful there, and it was a good place to think about what he was going to say later.

Few people ever visited the old churchyard and tower, mainly because it was so overgrown, and some would never go anywhere near the place because it was just plain scary.

Even in daylight, it was difficult not to let your imagination run away with you. The stories of its haunting were legendary. The most common story told by the locals was hearing the bells toll from the old tower at night, even though they had been removed to the new church 150 years ago.

Daniel made his way down the lane towards the old tower. Although he was sad to be burying an old friend, it was at times like this, the quiet times, the times when he was alone with nobody to bother him, that he had time to think. It was at times like this that he realised just how lucky he was to be living and working in such a peaceful and friendly village. It was a far cry from an army chaplain's career.

The Reverend Daniel Carter, Captain in Her Majesty's 2nd Battalion Parachute Regiment, had served with distinction in Afghanistan and on several tours of Northern Ireland. The memories of death were never far from his thoughts, as his nightmares constantly reminded him. Towards the end of his army career, he had begun to question his attitude, even his faith. It had all been so easy at the beginning. It was somehow easier to convince himself that the death of young soldiers was meaningful, but towards the end he found it difficult to reconcile his Christian beliefs with what he now regarded as the useless slaughter of young soldiers and civilians alike.

He recalled the memory of a young soldier who had lain fatally wounded in Helmand Province. He remembered holding him, telling him everything was all right but knowing that the young soldier's life was slowly ebbing from him. Only three months before, he had officiated at the soldier's wedding. On his return to England, he had visited his widow. Like every other person who has suffered the loss of a loved one taken prematurely from them, she asked, "Why? Why did he have to die?"

Daniel was finding it more and more difficult to give an answer, but when all else fails you can always fall back on the old chestnut: "God works in mysterious ways."

He felt anger and even guilt that in nearly twenty years of army life he had never been seriously hurt, and the only permanent injury he had ever received was whilst playing cricket for the regiment. A mistimed catch and the ball had struck his left ear, leaving him deaf and with an invitation to join civilian life.

Ethel Schneider knew how he felt. She never asked questions, but she knew and understood his pain. "You got lots of medals, must be difficult being a soldier and a vicar, eh Daniel?" she would say. He never did answer her. He never had to.

He remembered how she used to sing at the top of her voice, especially in the church; she always seemed so happy. Yet he was never certain that she was even a Christian. The consensus of village opinion was that she was probably Jewish, but he had never liked to ask. He supposed it was rather strange, Ethel cleaning and helping in a Christian church, but nobody ever mentioned it, probably because they did not want to upset her, and it made no difference anyway, because today she would be laid to rest with her beloved Bill and receive a full Christian service.

Daniel strolled along the lane that led to the old church tower. The site of the church was quite small since its destruction and the building of a much larger one. The tower and what remained of the church foundations were surrounded on all sides by high pointed iron railings, and the only way into the tower was via an iron gate with a large padlock and chain. As if that wasn't enough, the tower itself was protected by a large heavy oak door with an equally robust iron lock. Daniel couldn't image anyone wanting to go in there anyway.

The headstones surrounding the tower in this part of the cemetery were just as dilapidated as the tower itself. Yet although most of them were in a bad state and some broken, Daniel had noticed that some of them had been well cared for and the names of the inhabitants had been re-engraved on the stone.

He pushed back the bushes and made his way along the narrow path that led past the tower. Here too Mother Nature had taken over, covering the headstones and the names of those buried beneath.

"Why doesn't someone clear this place up?" he muttered to himself. "But you're a fine one to talk, Daniel. You can't even tackle your postage stamp of a garden."

It was then that he noticed a small black leather wallet lying just inside the railings. Strange, he thought. Not many people ventured in here. And then he saw the rolled-up magazine lying a few feet away. He turned to the centre pages, which revealed Miss April in an explicit full-frontal posture.

"I haven't seen you in my church, young lady," he murmured. "I would definitely have noticed you." He smiled to himself and looked around for signs of cigarette stubs. On a previous visit he had stumbled across some local boys smoking and smirking over porn magazines and guessed the same group were responsible, but there were no cigarette ends. He placed the magazine in his pocket, together with the black leather wallet. As he did so he saw the gold initials on one corner: *SJ*.

He continued to thread his way through the undergrowth towards his new church. Not that it was really new, but that was the way he thought of it and it was certainly better cared for than the grounds of the old church tower. He emerged into the cemetery through a gap in the large and recently-clipped hedge. This brought him out just behind the village war memorial, which stood at the top end of the burial ground, dividing as it did the old church from the new.

He stood in front of the memorial and read the names of the men and women from the village who had been killed in two world wars. It was something he always did when he came this way. Somehow he always expected to recognise some of the names. Perhaps their relatives were now members of his church and he didn't know it. At the bottom of the plinth were the names of an entire family, all civilians. The only bomb to drop on the village had wiped out three generations. The remains of the Remembrance Day wreaths still lay around the base of the plinth, the messages of love and thanksgiving washed away by the weather.

"What a waste. Such a damn waste!" He looked around and listened with his good ear and smiled to himself. "So quiet, so peaceful, you're a lucky man, Daniel Carter."

He listened; only the birds' morning chorus broke the silence. His wellbeing restored, he continued along the shale path towards the church. His eyes continued along the rows of clean upright headstones to the dark mound of freshly-dug earth which marked the spot where in a few hours Ethel would be laid to rest with her beloved husband.

He stopped and looked again at the mound of earth, almost in disbelief. The earth had been scattered across the shale path, its blackness standing out against the light grey of the path.

"Bloody foxes," he grunted. Then he stopped dead in his tracks.

Foxes didn't desecrate graves. Foxes didn't smash headstones.

He could not believe what his eyes were telling him. He ran to the edge of the grave, anger welling up inside him.

"You bastards!" he yelled, not caring who heard his outcry. "What bloody maniac has done this?"

The headstones of both William Schneider and the Reverend Winterbourne had been smashed, and red paint was daubed everywhere. Even the flint wall behind the graves was splattered, and the word "NO" was written on what remained of the headstone.

Daniel knelt at the side of the open grave, almost afraid to look in. His worst fears were realised when he saw that the remains of William Schneider's coffin had been smashed open and his skull lay on top like a trophy, the eye holes staring back at him. Daniel felt his stomach turn over. He was trembling with rage. On the forehead of the skull, in red paint, was again the word "NO".

He stood up and glared at the sight before him. He saw that the green tarpaulin which would be placed around the grave during the ceremony had been slung across the branch of a tree. He pulled on it, with the intention of laying it over the open grave to bring some sort of order and dignity. It was caught on something. He wasn't paying attention to what he was doing as his eyes were still staring into the open grave.

He gave the tarpaulin a firm tug and at once it unfolded, its contents spilling the bodily remains of William Schneider at his feet. The shock was instantaneous. His breath caught in his throat and he half choked on his own bile.

Daniel ran half-stumbling through the cemetery, towards Constable Bradley's police house, which was no more than two hundred yards away. He banged on the door with both fists and immediately Constable Bradley, a big man with slicked-back dark hair, appeared from his garage at the side.

"You frightened the living daylights out of me, vicar," he said.

"Help me, please help me!" gasped Daniel.

Chapter 2

Half a mile away on the outskirts of Etwell, Andrew Summers was preparing for the arrival of his two grandsons, Richard, aged nine, and James, two years younger. Once a year his daughter Sally would bring them over from France, where she lived with their father George. The pair of terrors would stay for two weeks, and it was the highlight of his year. It was made even more special for Andrew since the death of his wife Alison the year before. Andrew would never admit it, but he was very lonely.

He had spent weeks preparing for their arrival. The house was spotless, and the fridge and freezer were filled to overflowing with assorted goodies. He had even employed a local gardener to return his overgrown wilderness back to its former glory.

It wasn't that Andrew was lazy, far from it, but since Alison had died he had lost interest in nearly everything, including the garden. His only interest was his beloved daughter and his two grandchildren. They were his only reason for living.

After being invalided out of the fire service with a damaged knee joint, Andrew had looked forward to a happy retirement with his wife, who had been a teacher in the village primary school, a job she loved. They had been comfortably off financially, with a good pension, and were fortunate to live in a modest house that backed onto farmland and woods.

"You don't know how lucky you are," his daughter had often reminded him. She was right of course, but he still felt alone. His only companion now was Chester, his large Airedale Terrier. They spent many hours in the fields and woods at the back of the house. It was very convenient; they only had to walk to the end of the garden, open the gate in the back fence and there they were. It was like having your own private woods.

The area was steeped in history. King Henry the VIII had built his fabulous palace here, hence the name, 'Nonsuch', after Henry's Nonsuch Palace, because like the palace, there was nothing like it. The palace had long since gone of course, and the only reminders were three granite pillars that marked out its former position. Only a couple of hundred yards away lay the site of King Henry's banqueting hall, discovered in the 1960s when they were widening the road. Although the building had gone, the beautiful mosaic floor was still there.

Andrew always thought it sad that such an important historical site should be covered up with not even a sign to inform people of its existence. The area was totally overgrown. Andrew loved telling his grandsons about the gold coins that had been found. He had spent many happy days with them searching for buried treasure. Not that they ever found any – after all, this area had been searched by experts – but to two young boys it was a never-ending adventure, and to them Granddad was the cleverest man in the world.

In fact he even had a trophy to prove it. It was a big silver pot, which was always kept highly polished and took pride of place on a shelf in the lounge. The inscription on the trophy read "Andrew Summers, the World's First Tiddlywinks Champion." They were very proud of him and his achievement and had promised faithfully, a cross your heart and hope to die type of promise, never to touch Granddad's wonderful trophy. In reality the trophy was a tea urn with the spout turned to the wall. He was going to tell them it was the FA Cup, but as they knew more about football than he did, he felt on safer ground with tiddlywinks.

Andrew always phoned the boys once a week. He had delighted in teasing them about the wonderful surprise he had waiting for them when they arrived, saying they would have to wait.

When the dusty blue Volvo turned onto his driveway, it was laden with boxes, suitcases and two mountain bikes. Andrew rushed to the door just in time to see his beloved grandchildren leap from the car.

"Granddad, Granddad!" they shouted excitedly. For the next two weeks Andrew's quiet and lonely life would be turned upside down, and he couldn't wait.

"George not with you darling?" he said as he hugged his daughter.

"No, not this time Dad. You know how it is. He's just so busy."

Yes, I know exactly how it is, thought Andrew, but for the next two weeks George's name would not be mentioned. They had never got on together. The last time they had met was at James' christening. George hadn't even bothered to attend Alison's funeral but it pleased Andrew greatly to know that his three favourite people in the world were his for a whole two weeks, and he couldn't wait to get started.

Chapter 3

"But you promised!"

"Stephen's quite right, you did promise, and you know he's been going on about that film for ages."

"Look, I'm sorry. I must get these quotes ready. We'll go tomorrow, Stephen."

"That's no good, the film ends today. I've been on holiday for a week, not that you noticed."

"Now that's not fair, Stephen. You know your father has been very busy."

"Yes I know I promised, but I must finish this work today. I'll take you tomorrow."

"Stephen has just told you the film ends today!" The anger in her voice was evident, and Brian Jennings knew his twelve-year-old son was not going to forgive him easily, nor was his long-suffering wife.

They were in fact a happy family, with a nice if modest home, but since the recession finances were very tight and job security a thing of the past.

Mr Jennings' temper finally snapped. "For Christ sake! He's nearly thirteen. Can't he go on his own?"

"No he can't, and don't talk like that in front of Stephen."

"Thanks a lot, father."

It was now Stephen's turn to be sarcastic. He walked towards the open kitchen door, grabbed his bike, which was just outside, and disappeared from view.

"Have you got enough money, darling?" Mrs Jennings called after him.

"Don't worry about me, mother, I can look after myself."

Stephen pushed his bike along the road towards the town centre, the anger and bitterness he felt towards his parents causing his eyes to water.

"At least mum could have come. Who needs them anyway?" he grumbled

Just then a shiny black Mercedes estate drew up alongside Stephen. On the door panel was written in gold lettering, JESUS SAVES. Obviously the driver was about to ask him for directions.

Chapter 4

"I saw more of you when you were in army than I do now," sobbed Lucy.

"Oh, so it's my bloody fault now is it? You were bored so you found yourself a boyfriend."

"You bastard! David is not my boyfriend. He lost his wife last year."

"So he thought you could take her place in his bed?"

"Malcolm, it was nothing like that!"

"Well you looked very cosy together. And why him for Christ's sake, a fucking woodentop?"

"That's it isn't it? You can't stand the fact that he's a uniformed officer and not one of your wonderful CID. Well, for your information I didn't even know he was a police officer until you burst in."

"How long have you been seeing him?"

"I see him every day when I take our boys to school. Do you remember your boys? They're the two children upstairs, the ones you have never taken to school, not even on their first day. You've never been to sports days or open evenings."

"I do actually work for a bloody living!"

"And don't we know it! Yes, down the pub with your CID mates, all calling you 'guv'. You swopped one boys' club for another. What about us?"

"You can do what you damn well like, I don't give a shit any more."

"Where are you going, for god's sake? We have to talk about this. We were having lunch that's all, don't go. I'm sorry, but don't go."

"I'll let you know where I'm staying," he said bitterly and slammed the door behind him.

Detective Inspector Malcolm Cammock climbed into his car and sat for a moment before starting the engine. The pain and anger he felt welled up inside him, and as he steered his car out of the driveway, tears began to stream down his cheeks.

Chapter 5

As expected, the church was filled to overflowing, not just with friends and villagers who had come to pay their last respects but with the press, and not just the local papers but even the nationals had got hold of the story. If that wasn't bad enough, the church was bristling with TV cameras and there were cables running all over the place. It was obviously a quiet news day, because the desecration of the graves had made the national news, and the press had already decided that this was an anti-semitic attack. The village of Etwell had been swamped by reporters and photographers tramping over the cemetery, and Daniel was not best pleased. He tried to remain calm by telling himself they were just doing their job, but when three young hacks barged into his vestry while he was changing and preparing for Ethel's funeral, they got more than they bargained for. Dan the man lived up to his reputation, and even they were shocked by his uncompromising manner. Unfortunately for Daniel, his outburst had been heard by the entire congregation waiting in the church.

Even during the ceremony photographers were clicking away with their cameras at anyone who looked remotely interesting. It was when Daniel climbed into the pulpit to deliver his eulogy that he finally lost his temper. There laid out on the floor were several microphones.

Daniel stopped the service. Then he seized two of the recording devices and held them aloft.

"I want these removed from my church immediately!" he boomed. Several reporters shuffled forward, looking rather embarrassed. He pointed directly at the group of cameramen and reporters who had gathered at the back of the church. "I want you lot out of my church!" he shouted. "Yes you, all of you, get out! This is not your newsroom. This is a house of God. These people have come here to pay their last respects. I can't control what goes on outside, but inside I can and I will!" He glared at the assembled press corps.

It was the sight of Constable Vincent Bradley's massive frame rising from one of the front pews that made sure Daniel's order was carried out. It would be a very foolish man who argued with Constable Bradley this day.

The media men and women shuffled out of the church and Daniel began his service by asking the congregation to stand and sing Psalm 23, The Lord Is My Shepherd, which had been one of Ethel's favourites.

As the congregation rose he noticed a young female reporter had dropped her camera. He was about to say something when he realised that he remembered her from the fete the day before. He had even promised her an interview. She looked up at him, and he smiled back reassuringly. What was her name? Daniel racked his brains. Either way he found her rather attractive.

When the funeral was over Daniel stood by the grave whilst the mourners filed passed, some of them dropping flowers onto the coffin. When they had all gone, he made his way back slowly towards the vestry. Just then he saw the woman reporter walking off along the lane, and he managed to catch her eye. He waved and smiled, and she waved back.

"See you tomorrow," she called.

Daniel's quiet contemplation of his reporter, whose name he was still struggling to remember, was interrupted by Constable Bradley's large hand gently resting on his shoulder.

"That was a nice service Dan, and a good turnout,"

said the officer. "Apart from those arseholes! Sorry Dan. Fancy a drink?"

"Don't apologise. You're right and yes, I would love a drink. Give me five minutes to get changed and I'll join you in Tommy's, and by the way, thanks for all your help, er... this morning." Daniel's voice tailed off.

"Don't mention it. The lads didn't take long to do their forensic stuff, not that there was much anyway, and well, everyone wanted to help get the place cleaned up. I'm off for a couple of days. So if there's anything else I can do?"

"Most of it's done now, but thanks anyway."

"By the way Dan, you do realise the pub is full of press each trying to win a Pulitzer Prize? "

"Forget that then, we'll go back to the cottage. I've got plenty of wine and beer."

Daniel saw the raised eyebrows and Bradley's wry smile.

"All kindly denoted by my grateful parishioners, I'll have you know." He removed his clerical collar, folded his robes and placed them neatly in the cupboard.

They passed by the grave of Bill and Ethel Schneider, which had been covered with fresh flowers. The headstones had been removed and only slight traces of red paint remained on the flint wall. They both paused for a moment, each with their own thoughts.

"You know Daniel, I never knew they were Jewish."

"What do you mean?"

"Well, I can't think of any other reason for someone to do this."

"Neither can I. But I never knew either. I always presumed they were Christian, what with working for the church all those years."

One glance around Daniel's cottage was enough to tell a visitor that he desperately needed a new housekeeper. Vincent Bradley stood in the middle of the lounge and looked around. "I've been in better squats than this, Daniel," he said as he cleared a pile of washing from a chair and sat down.

"I'm so sorry. Since Ethel, I really haven't had time." Daniel looked around the room. It was then that he realised just how far he had let things slide. His lounge really was a dump.

"Ethel looked after you well, didn't she?"

"And why not? She was used to looking after single vicars."

"How do you make that out? She never worked for Winterbourne, only you."

"Do you know, that's amazing! I always thought she had. She often spoke about him. I just presumed..."

"You must be joking. Old Reverend Winterbourne never allowed anyone near the place, apart from Bill."

"Well how come I got Ethel? Not that I'm complaining."

"We were all a bit surprised. She'd never shown any interest in the church before. Most of us thought it was her way of being close to her old man. You do know her husband was killed in that fire next door?"

"Yes, that must have been awful," replied Daniel. At the same time he was gathering up his dirty washing and various old newspapers which were strewn around the room.

Bradley was right; it did look like a squat. Daniel looked around for somewhere to put the pile of clothes and decided to dump the lot behind the door. "I'll sort it out later," he said. He went into the kitchen and returned shortly with two open bottles of wine. He placed them down and settled back.

"I've always wanted to ask you a question, Vince," said Daniel as he poured the wine.

"Fire away, Daniel."

"Was it true that your father hid Bill and Ethel in his police house during the war? You know, when the authorities were looking for them."

"I'm sorry to say it is true. To be honest I never had much time for either of them. Nice drop of wine that," said Bradley, draining his glass and changing the subject at the same time.

Daniel realised that it was probably expedient not to continue on that particular subject.

The more wine they consumed, the more relaxed and

chatty they became. The first two bottles of wine were drunk very quickly. Daniel rose, and with just a hint of unsteadiness he went into the kitchen for replacements.

"Do you know Dan, you're one of the most unlikely vicars I've ever met," said Bradley as he watched Daniel return and place two more bottles of wine on the table.

"And you, Constable Bradley, are the biggest bloody policeman I've ever come across."

"That's what I mean. Vicars don't normally swear."

"Don't they?"

"And they don't read porn magazines." Bradley waved the magazine in front of him triumphantly and laughed at the embarrassment he was causing his drinking companion.

"Oh that!" said Daniel. "I can explain that."

"I bet you can."

"No honestly. I found that by the old tower this morning."

"Of course you did Dan," replied Bradley mockingly.

"No it's true. You can trust me, I'm a vicar."

Both men started laughing, but then the black wallet slipped out from between the pages of the magazine.

"I suppose this isn't yours either?"

"No. I found that by the tower as well."

"What were you doing up by the tower anyway?"

"Why shouldn't I be there? It's my bloody tower." The effects of the drink and the fact that it had been a long and traumatic day were beginning to take their toll on Daniel.

"There you go again. Vicars shouldn't swear, and anyway the tower is haunted, everyone knows that."

"You don't actually believe that, do you?"

"Of course not, but my father used to frighten the living daylights out of the people round here with his stories."

"What stories?"

"Oh you know, the sounds of screaming, the bells ringing in the middle of the night, that sort of thing. Then there were the three workmen who worked for one day and then refused to go back inside the tower. They said they could hear voices, and that was only a few years ago. No Daniel my old friend, most people won't go anywhere near the old tower."

Constable Bradley realised that he had been talking to himself. Daniel had drifted off into a deep sleep. Bradley stood up and placed a blanket that had been on the floor over his slumbering friend. Then he placed the magazine and wallet in his pocket and left quietly.

Chapter 6

Andrew Summers came down the stairs two at a time. "Where are the boys?" he called to Sally, who was busy in the kitchen.

"They've been up for hours. That metal detector was a wonderful idea of yours. They're thrilled with it." Sally met her father in the hall and kissed him on the cheek. "Thanks, Dad. I haven't seen them this excited for ages."

"Well I hope they won't be too disappointed when they don't unearth the Crown Jewels."

"I suppose they're all right on their own?" asked Sally.

"They're not on their own, Chester is with them and nobody is going to harm those boys while he is around, so don't worry on that score. I'll have a quick cup of tea and go and help them find the treasure."

Andrew was too late. Richard and James had already found the buried treasure, without his help. He had always told them that King Henry's treasure was buried nearby, and now they had found it. They were going to be rich, and granddad would not have to live on his own any more.

The metal detector had gone right off the dial. A strong high-pitched bleep was registering over a plot the size of a small door.

"It must be a treasure chest at the very least," said Richard excitedly. James was jumping up and down with sheer delight.

The ground was soft and quite muddy, but Richard and James didn't care about the mud. It actually made their job easier. They pushed their trowels into the soil. Even Chester was interested and started sniffing, but was pushed away by the boys.

"It's metal!" cried James. "I've struck metal. It *is* a treasure chest!"

Richard, being the elder, took charge. "Be careful. It might be a bomb."

James stopped digging at once. "Can you feel it? Use your hands."

Both boys thrust their hands beneath the surface.

"I've got it!" said James.

"So have I. Pull together. One, two, three..."

Both boys pulled with all their might, but what emerged from beneath the shallow pit was not buried treasure.

"It's just an old bike," groaned James. "That's really stupid. Who would want to bury a bike?"

But his brother was wiping the mud off the frame, and bright red paintwork began to appear. His eyes suddenly lit up. "Hey James, this bike is almost brand new. Look! It's a Claude Butler!"

"Wow! Perhaps it's stolen and the robbers will come back and get it when the coast is clear," said James.

The boys fell silent and looked around them. This was serious. Time to get Granddad. He would know what to do.

But their grandfather was already coming through the woods to find them. "Richard, James! Where are you?"

"Over here Granddad. Come quickly! We've found something. Hurry!"

Andrew smiled to himself. "More treasure! I just don't know how I do it."

The sight of Richard and James standing either end of a mud-covered bike and smiling from ear to ear was not what he had expected to see.

"Where on earth did you find that?"

"Just over there. We've just dug it up, it's brand new and it's a Claude Butler!" said James.

"Honestly Granddad, it was buried over there," said Richard. "James thought it was buried treasure, but I think it's stolen and the thieves will return for it as soon as the coast is clear."

James' mouth dropped open. "That's what I said."

Granddad saw the look on Richard's face and guessed that it was probably not an original idea.

"Let's go and check it out, but we must be careful," he whispered. "It might be booby trapped."

He smiled and dropped to the ground. The boys dropped the bike and followed suit. All three crawled commando-style towards where they had found the bike.

"Watch out for any mines, and be careful of snakes, they could be deadly," said Andrew. He had to admit it, he hadn't had this much fun for ages. The boys for their part were only too pleased to join in yet another adventure, while Chester stood guard.

Granddad and his two brave commandos began to crawl through the snake-infested grass, carefully avoiding the mines that lay beneath them. James knew it was just a game, but he still looked nervously at the grass, just in case Granddad was serious about the snakes.

Granddad peered into the hole. He carefully started removing the soil.

"It's looks like a plastic ground sheet of some sort," he said.

"Pull the sheet off, Granddad."

"Yes come on Granddad. There might be another bike underneath."

All three stood up and Granddad reached in and grabbed a corner of the sheet.

"Presenting... Granddad!' said Richard. 'The most famous magician in the whole world will now produce for you..."

Andrew threw back the sheet, watching the boys' faces for their reaction, but James just stood transfixed, his eyes staring into the pit. Richard had gone white. He vomited uncontrollably and tumbled back, dragging his younger brother with him. Even Chester recoiled from the scene.

Andrew looked into the hole. There before him lay the mud-caked body of a young boy curled up in a foetal position. He was entirely naked.

George collected his children the same day, having flown direct from Paris. The boys clung tightly to either side of their mother in the back of the car as they drove out of the driveway. George's parting words to him were,

"That's the last time my children ever visit you."

The words kept spinning around in Andrew's head. He would never forget the sight of that poor boy and the numbness he felt. Andrew suddenly felt very old and alone again, but he was also very, very angry.

AUSTIN GREEN

Chapter 7

Daniel slowly opened his eyes. He felt cold and shivery, his throat was dry and the constant throbbing in his head only went to remind him that all his ills were self-inflicted.

"How much did we drink?" he muttered. He turned to face his drinking partner, but Vincent Bradley had long gone. Only the empty bottles and glasses were left to remind him, as if he needed reminding, of the previous night's binge.

As Daniel's head began to clear, the memory of the funeral and the shock and anger he had felt at finding the desecrated graves came back. Not to mention his run-in with the media and of course, to add insult to injury, his bout of heavy drinking with Constable Bradley.

"Why do I do it?" he groaned. Bradley was right,

this place was a dump. He looked at his reflection in the mirror that hung over the fireplace. "You're a bloody disgrace, Captain Carter. Get your act together," he barked in a sergeant-major voice.

He turned away from his reflection and ran his fingers through his hair. He looked around the room once more. This wasn't just yesterday's mess. He hadn't done a stroke since Ethel had died, and the place was beginning to smell.

Daniel looked into the mirror once more. The house wasn't the only thing that needed sorting out. Coffee and a shower first, and then he would damn well get this place cleaned up. Yes sir! He saluted his reflection and walked through to the kitchen. His bare feet stuck to the floor like sticky tape. The sink was full of dirty dishes and several half-empty foil trays from the Indian restaurant in the village.

"They've probably put their kids through private school with all the money I've spent in there recently," he muttered.

He opened the fridge door and reached for the milk. The rancid smell attacked his senses. Black coffee. That was what he needed and lots of it. He filled the kettle and switched it on. He looked down at the dark suit trousers that now hung over his bare feet like tents. His white shirt was unbuttoned to the waist, and a large wine stain adorned the front. A shower first. He had to have a shower.

Daniel returned to the kitchen after his shower feeling suitably refreshed, with only a hint of his headache still remaining and carrying a large bundle of washing. He had changed into tracksuit bottoms and a white T-shirt. He pulled a mug from the pile of dirty crockery and wiped it with the apron that now hung round his waist.

"Right, let's get cracking," he muttered. He opened the washing machine and pushed a large pile of clothes into it, but he had to open several cupboards before he could find the washing powder under the sink. He then poured hot water into the sink and added the washing-up liquid. He left them to soak while he emptied the fridge of all its rotten and out of date contents and piled them into a large black plastic sack. Then, with military efficiency, he went through every room in the cottage gathering up all his scattered clothes, glasses, cups, plates, saucers and other belongings that had been abandoned, depending on which room he was in at the time.

When each room had been vacuumed and polished he threw open the windows, the first time that had been done in a while. It was mid-afternoon by the time he'd finished. He had even lit the coal fire in the lounge.

He was just finishing off the kitchen floor when the doorbell rang. He dried his hands on his apron and went through the hall to the front door.

"No. I'm not coming out to play, you drunken policeman," he grumbled.

Daniel flung open the door. As he did so he held his apron in front of his face. "I don't want any comments from you, I'm still recovering."

"Reverend Carter! It is you?"

Daniel lowered the apron.

"Ah Miss April. May. June. Miss Walsh. I'm so sorry. You must think I'm a complete idiot. I was expecting someone else. Please come in."

"You did remember I was coming today?"

"Oh yes of course." Daniel stood back and ushered June Walsh into the hall. He couldn't help but notice the tight jeans she was wearing and how they accentuated her form. She wasn't a slim woman, but she had a great figure.

"Please go through to the lounge, Miss Walsh. I think you'll find it more comfortable."

"A coal fire! How lovely, and at this time of year as well."

"Make yourself at home. I'll go and put the coffee on. I'm afraid it will have to be black, I've run out of milk."

"Black's fine," she called after him as he disappeared into the kitchen.

June Walsh studied the photographs that were displayed on the mantelpiece. She particularly liked the one of her host being presented to Prince Charles – it would make a good piece for her article – and another of him dressed in combat gear surrounded by his fellow Paras all armed to the teeth with automatic weaponry and him in the middle wearing his clerical collar and holding a prayer book. It was an unlikely combination.

"But a good-looking combination," murmured Miss Walsh to herself. "Even heavenly, you might say." She smiled and thought how she might work that into her storyline.

Daniel returned with a tray. "Do you take sugar, Miss Walsh? It appears that I haven't quite grasped the principles of shopping yet. I left all that sort of thing to Ethel."

"No thanks, and please call me June."

"Thanks, and you must call me Dan."

He placed the tray on the table between them and handed her a cup of coffee.

"I hope you won't think I'm being condescending Dan, but I really am impressed by the way you keep your home. Most men wouldn't know one end of a duster from the other and to be honest, I thought after Ethel passed away you would have got someone else in by now."

"Well I'm in the honesty business myself, and I thought it would be nice to look after myself for a change."

"Well if you don't mind my saying, the last thing I expected was you wearing an apron! You don't act or dress like any other vicar I've met."

"You know it's strange, somebody said exactly that only yesterday."

They smiled at each other, although Daniel knew it was not for the same reason. He recalled Ethel saying, "If my vicar ever looks you straight in the eyes and says something is so, then he's probably lying."

"A nice thing to say about anyone, especially when he's a vicar," said June.

Dan felt very at ease in her company and relaxed back into his armchair.

"Now what would you like to know, June?"

"Well to start with, do you mind if I record this? It's so much easier than making notes. I promise I will let you read my copy before it's printed."

"You can't be fairer than that."

Dan refilled their cups and settled back. He talked about his early army career, the loss of his parents in a road crash, whilst serving abroad, his delight and surprise at getting his present job, and of course his feelings over the events of yesterday.

"You will stop me if I go rabbiting on won't you, June?"

"Stop you? You've only filled the centre pages so far!"

Bleep, bleep, bleep... The sound of June's pager interrupted their conversation.

"Oh damn! I'm so sorry Dan. I was forgetting where

I was for a moment. I've got this old bleeper because I managed to drop my mobile in the bath."

"Don't worry about that. They always go off at the wrong time, don't they? If you want to use the phone, it's in the hall. I'll make some more coffee."

June was disappointed at the interruption. She was enjoying Daniel's company very much indeed, and not just because he was going to make a fascinating story. In fact she couldn't remember anyone else whose company she had enjoyed as much.

Daniel was in the kitchen pouring out the fresh coffee when June burst in.

"I'm sorry Dan, I won't have time for coffee. That was my editor. They've just found a body up by the Old Banqueting Hall and they want me to cover it," she said excitedly. "It's not often we get the drop on the nationals."

"Well, bully for you!" Daniel said angrily. He made no attempt to hide his disgust at her attitude towards someone else's tragedy.

"Look Dan, I'm sorry. I didn't mean that the way it sounded."

"Apology accepted," said Daniel reluctantly. "Leave your car here. We can take the short cut down Drovers Alley. You never know, they might even need my services."

"Oh hell! I haven't got my camera."

June was about to apologise yet again, but Daniel smiled and took his own digital camera from the kitchen drawer. He placed it in her hands. "Will this do?"

The area had already being taped off by police when Daniel and June emerged from Drovers Alley, which was directly across the road from the Old Banqueting Hall. They crossed the road to where a small crowd had gathered. Almost immediately a young policeman stepped forward.

"You can't go any further, miss."

"I'm from the press," said June, flourishing her press card in front of him.

"Well you definitely can't go any further then."

Daniel thought, he might be young, but he spoke with authority and he has the same opinion of the press as I do.

"Can you just tell me what has happened? Is it a murder? Do you know who it is yet?"

The officer looked at June. His previously expressionless face had changed to one of impatience and annoyance.

"Just go away please, madam," he said.

June moved along the tape so that she could be nearer a group of men who were standing about twenty yards away. Some of them were dressed in white overalls with cellophane bags on their feet; others wore suits and were deep in conversation.

"It's definitely a murder. That's Chief Superintendent Wilkes over there."

"You're really enjoying this, aren't you?" said Daniel.

June pretended she hadn't heard him, and using the bushes as cover, she made her way closer and closer to what looked like a shallow grave. She clicked away with her borrowed camera as she drew nearer. Daniel stayed where he was. He wanted nothing to do with what he regarded as a tasteless exhibition.

"This is great. I can see right into the hole," she murmured, adjusting the zoom lens of the camera. "These are going to be great shots."

"Get that bloody women out of here!" shouted a loud male voice. A heavy-set man came across the ground to where June was hiding in the bushes. But through the viewfinder, she had already seen the contents of the shallow grave.

Daniel had been watching her and felt nothing but contempt at her seeming lack of respect. He saw her start to run back towards him. She stumbled across the uneven ground, white with shock. Her hand was clasped tightly over her mouth. She collapsed into his arms, crying and ashen faced.

"It's a boy. Just a little boy!" she said before she fainted.

The small crowd that had gathered gasped when they heard her pathetic words.

"I'm sorry sir," said the young policeman, putting a hand out for the camera.

Daniel handed the camera to the officer. He didn't care about the camera or its contents. His only concern was June.

Then a man who had been standing impassively at the rear of the crowd stepped forward; Andrew Summers. "Bring her to my house. I live just over there." He pointed along a small path that led to a garden. "Chester, heel boy!" The large Airedale Terrier moved swiftly at his command.

Chapter 8

Within hours of the gruesome discovery, a murder squad office had been set up. Detectives from all parts of South London were drafted in, together with computer operators and civilian staff. No murder investigation could do without computers, and this investigation would be no different.

Detective Chief Superintendent Wilkes from the major investigation unit was in overall charge. He was a man of nearly thirty years' experience, over twenty of those in CID. He was the first to admit that he knew very little about computers, but he understood their value, especially in major crimes such as this. However, being 'old school' and proud of it, he insisted that everything was backed up with the old-fashioned card index system.

Wilkes was a quietly spoken man, but those officers who had worked under him recognised his immense knowledge and respected him because he got the job done and he did not suffer fools under any circumstances, This, together with his dry sense of humour, made him ideal for the task that lay ahead of him.

The day-to-day running of the investigation was to be handled by Malcolm Cammock. He had ten years' experience and had risen through the ranks quickly to Detective Inspector. His past experience in army intelligence and his university background had made him an ideal candidate for accelerated promotion.

One of the most important jobs in any major investigation is that of office manager. This task had been assigned to Detective Sergeant Claire Billings, a woman of enormous experience and a wicked sense of humour. Every day for the past ten months she had religiously crossed the day off her calendar. She had just forty-five days to go before retiring with her husband to pastures new, and she couldn't wait.

The large conference room that was being used was already buzzing with activity, and people were busy setting up the office equipment. In the centre, several smaller tables had been pushed together to form one large rectangular one. Other tables were placed against a wall, where banks of computers were already being set up. More telephones were installed. A smaller table was sited at one end and Claire Billings was already arranging her desk. In pride of place was her calendar, which she placed in full view on the notice board behind her desk. A message on the board read: "Office meeting 6 pm NO FAIL!"

On another much larger noticeboard the names of all investigating officers were being written up in black marker pen, followed by the officers' ranks and home and mobile telephone numbers.

One by one officers arrived and started to sift through the information that had already been gathered. Most of the officers were CID and had dealt with several murder cases before, but to PC Alan Shaw, who had been seconded from the local crime squad, it was a totally new experience.

"Right, ladies and gentlemen, let's make a start," said Detective Chief Superintendent Wilkes as he strode into the room. The officers sat themselves down around the big table. Some of them took out notebooks.

"For those of you who have never worked with me before, I just want to lay down a few ground rules. There will be no drinking while you are working. We work hard and play afterwards. Contrary to popular belief, murders are not solved by chief superintendents, or DCs come to that. They are solved by the painstaking work of gathering information, and that's your job. I don't give a damn if the station cleaner solves this one. I want a result."

He paused for a moment and looked around the table. He had known most of his officers for some time, and they likewise knew him. His gaze fell on Alan Shaw.

"It's Alan isn't it?"

"That's right sir."

"Well Alan, I run a fine system. Now I know the job frown on that sort of thing, but I don't give a damn. It means that if anyone is late for the daily meetings or fails to complete enquiries properly or any other infringement that either I, DI Cammock or DS Billings deem worthy of a fine it will be implemented, and there is no appeal. Is there anyone here who objects to my system?"

All the officers were laughing and grinning, all except Alan, who nervously raised his hand.

"How much will the fine be sir, only I'm getting married in a few weeks?"

"Don't worry son, with the overtime you're going to be earning, you can afford it," said an officer amid roars of laughter.

"Norman, you're fined for interrupting."

The team laughed even more as DC Norman Harris swung round in his chair to face his DI. "Way ahead of you boss," he said, producing a bottle of Jameson's Irish Whiskey from under the table.

"I take it it's still a green top." He grinned.

Both men joined in the laughter. DC Norman Harris had known his DI since long before he had joined the police force. In fact Norman liked to think that it was through his encouragement that his old friend had joined in the first place. They had first met in Northern Ireland, when Norman had been working with the Anti-Terrorist Squad and Malcolm had been a captain in army intelligence. In their dangerous undercover world, the two men had formed a strong bond of mutual respect.

"Right, let's settle down," said Chief Superintendent Wilkes. We've got a lot to do before any of us go home tonight. Have we had the pathologist's report back yet?"

"Not yet sir. He's starting at 9 am tomorrow. His initial findings however are that the boy had been raped more than once. There are signs of tearing on the anal wall, but the actual cause of death we'll know tomorrow."

Sergeant Claire Billings closed the notebook she had been reading from and then added, "It's possible sir, but unconfirmed, that the boy bled to death."

The murmurings of revulsion and disgust came from all sides of the table.

"Right, let's start off by giving our boy a name."

Mr Wilkes looked at Norman. "You've been to see the family."

"Stephen Jennings. He is, or was, the only son of Brian and Linda. He would have been thirteen in two weeks' time. The bike, although it hasn't been positively identified, was bought as an early birthday present for him. His parents reported him missing at about seven o'clock on Sunday evening. Stephen apparently left the house at about 2.30 pm after a row with his father. Dad had promised to take him to the pictures but was too busy. I've done the basic checks on the family and there is nothing known. In all they strike me as your average family. At the moment they are completely shell shocked, and mum has been sedated.

"The body was found at about nine o'clock this morning by two youngsters using a metal detector. They are over here from France visiting their grandfather. He had bought them the metal detector as a present, and that's how they uncovered the bike. The boy was buried in the shallow grave with a plastic sheet placed over him and the bike was on top."

"Thanks Norman. What about statements?"

"In hand for tomorrow, guv."

"Who's going to the post mortem tomorrow, Claire?" said Mr Wilkes. "Any volunteers?"

Alan raised his hand. "I've never been to one. I don't mind going."

"Rather you than me. I bloody hate them. I always throw up."

"What else is happening, Claire?"

"The TSG are doing house to house and I've arranged

for the area to be patrolled for the next few days to prevent the ghouls from appearing."

"Right, I want a complete background on Stephen's parents, friends, teachers or anyone else who knew him. I want all the cinemas checked to see if he actually saw his film. I want all his friends spoken to. Does he belong to a club or anything? What are his hobbies? Has he got a girlfriend?" Mr Wilkes rattled off his instructions without drawing breath. "Anyone got any ideas? Come on, don't worry if it sounds stupid."

"The files on all known weirdos," said one officer.

"What about any other kids that might have gone missing?" said another.

"What about FIB? They might have something."

"Good thinking, make a note of that Claire and check with general registry."

"What about SO5, guv? They might have something."

The suggestions came thick and fast. Alan Shaw listened to these experienced officers with great admiration and only wished that he too could think of something intelligent to say. His thoughts were interrupted by Mr Wilkes.

"OK son get your coat on. I'll buy you a drink." Alan felt very privileged.

"What about the rest of us guv? You not buying us one as well?" said Norman.

"You're too old to drink, and anyway you've got an

early start in the morning looking after Alan here, at the post mortem."

Once again the team erupted with laughter. None of the team knew it, but that feeling of bonhomie was to be tested to the full over the coming days.

Chapter 9

When they arrived at Andrew Summers' house, Daniel and June followed Andrew through to the lounge. "Sit her on the couch," said Andrew. "I'll get some coffee and brandy."

Andrew disappeared into the kitchen, and when he returned June was sitting on the couch, sobbing quietly onto Daniel's shoulder. Daniel had comforted people many times before, that was the nature of his job, but perhaps it was June's vulnerability, and of course the fact that she was very attractive, that brought out his protective side.

Andrew crouched in front of her and gently pressed a glass of brandy into her hand.

"It's OK June. I know what you were thinking."

"I thought it was Derek." She sobbed even more, and Daniel placed his arm around her shoulder and drew her closer.

"It's all right, I understand," said Andrew. "Drink up, it'll make you feel better."

"You know each other then?" said Daniel, accepting the outstretched glass of brandy.

"I've known June since the day she was born. My late wife used to teach her and her brother in the village. Derek was June's brother."

Andrew stopped in mid-sentence, realising that he was awakening old memories in June that she might well prefer to forget.

"It's all right, Mr Summers. This is the Reverend Carter, you can tell him," said June. Wiping the tears from her face, she sat up and moved slightly away from Daniel as though she was embarrassed at their closeness, but Daniel still had his arm placed gently around her shoulders while she sipped her brandy.

"Yes, I remember you," said Andrew. "You conducted the service for my late wife's funeral last year. I'm Andrew Summers. It was my grandsons who discovered the body."

The men shook hands.

"Those poor boys. It must have been a terrible shock for them. Where are they now?" said Daniel.

"Their father flew over from France and took them back." Andrew did not bother to hide his sadness.

"I know how much you were looking forward to seeing them," said June.

Andrew handed mugs of coffee to his guests and replenished their glasses. "Derek would have been in his late twenties by now," he said.

"He was nearly eleven when he went missing," replied June.

Daniel squeezed her shoulder a little harder. "I'm sorry. I didn't know."

"There's no reason why you should," said Andrew. "My wife was one of the last people to see him alive. He was on his way home from school. He could have only been a few hundred yards from your cottage, vicar."

"I don't understand," queried Daniel. "Did you used to live near the vicarage?"

"I'm sorry Daniel. I should have made it clear from the start. I was actually born in the cottage you're living in now," said June, rolling the brandy glass between her fingers. "My parents sold it not long after Derek went missing. The church bought it, or to be more accurate the Reverend Winterbourne's family bought it. They're a very wealthy family, you know."

"June's father used to do a few odd jobs around the church if Bill was too busy digging his graves," said Andrew.

"Do you and your parents still live in Etwell?"

June lowered her head. Daniel looked at June and realised he had put his foot in it once again.

"Look, I'm sorry. I've obviously said the wrong thing again."

June smiled at him. "It's all right Dan. You weren't to know."

"About a year after Derek's disappearance, June's mother committed suicide," said Andrew.

"My mother never came to terms with what happened," said June. "My father was devastated at losing Derek, but when my mother died he just fell apart. He turned to drink. He lost his job, or rather nobody would employ him, and he just used to go off for days, sometimes weeks at a time. Then about five years ago he simply left the house and never came back. He was found frozen to death on a bench on the embankment opposite St Thomas's Hospital. So I'm all that's left of my family. I know in my heart that Derek is dead, but I can't forget. I think counsellors call it closure. I need to put Derek to rest in more ways than one."

"How awful for you," Daniel shook his head and held her tighter. "I had no idea."

"It all happened a long time before you came here." June smiled as if acknowledging his attention and was grateful for it. "The whole village helped with the search. It was run from the church hall. The police, even the army were called in to help, but we never found a trace of him."

"I suppose seeing that poor boy today up by the Banqueting Hall brought it all back," said Daniel, immediately thinking what a stupid thing that was to say.

"He was so small, so alone, so..." Andrew's voice tailed off. After a pause, he began to recount the story of how his grandsons had found the bike buried on top of the boy's body, the shocking effect it had had on both of them and the reaction of their father when he had collected them.

"If only I hadn't bought that damn metal detector," he grunted.

"Have they identified the boy yet?" said June, draining the last of her coffee.

"I heard one of the police constables say it was a boy from the other side of the village called Stephen Jennings. His parents had reported him missing."

"Those poor people. What must they be going through?" said Daniel.

"Do you mind if I use your phone Andrew?" asked June. "Only I'd better ring my editor. At this rate we'll be the last people with the story. No exclusive for us. Then I must go and pick my car up."

"Are you sure you want to do that?" enquired Daniel sympathetically. But her reply was not what he was expecting at all.

"Look, I know you don't like what I do and you probably think I'm a mercenary bitch, but someone has to pay the bills. Unlike some children left on their own, my parents left me nothing. Now I might not have a lot, but what I've got I intend to keep."

"I'm sorry if I gave you the impression that I disapproved. All I meant was that it's beginning to rain and you might like Andrew to call you a cab."

"Ah!" said June, feeling very embarrassed. "That would be nice. Thank you."

When June had rung her editor, she rejoined them in the lounge. Andrew refilled their coffee cups, and while he went outside to phone for a taxi, she continued her story about her brother and the effect his disappearance had had on her family.

"Dad continued to search for Derek long after the police had given up, but when mum went, he went downhill very fast. He just couldn't cope. Before it all happened we were a nice loving, hard-working family. The only time I ever saw my father take a drink was at Christmas."

The taxi sounded its horn and they all got up. She kissed Andrew on the cheek.

"Thanks for everything," she said.

He held her for a moment and kissed the top of her head. "Dan will see you out. I'll get some more coffee."

Daniel was glad of the opportunity to speak to June

in private. "Look, I'm sorry about before. Can I cook you a meal tonight to make up for it?"

"You cook as well!" said June mockingly as she made her down the driveway towards the waiting taxi. "Sounds great, thank you."

"Eight o'clock all right?" he called after her. "Perhaps we can finish that interview."

He wondered how old she was, reflecting that he was probably too old for her.

Daniel returned to the lounge just as Andrew was topping up his glass of brandy.

"Hold on Andrew. I haven't recovered from last night yet."

"Holding a wake, were you?"

"Yes, I'm afraid I fell in with bad company. Do you know Vincent Bradley? He's the local policeman."

"I bet he didn't need much arm twisting."

Both men laughed and settled down once more.

"Did you know Ethel Schneider?" asked Andrew.

"I knew her and her husband. In fact I was called in on the night of the fire. You do know about the fire in the vicarage?"

"I can't help but know, I live next door to it. Were you in the police or something?"

"I was a senior investigator with the fire service. I retired two years ago with ill health and my wife died a year later. The only company I have now is my dog and my grandsons, and I won't be seeing much more of them, if their father has his way. He thinks I'm very irresponsible, and he's probably right."

"I'm sure things will work out in time. But changing the subject slightly, it's always puzzled me about the old vicarage, why they never rebuilt it."

"It's not strange at all Dan, It's very simple really. The insurance company wouldn't pay up. The whole thing was dodgy from the start."

Daniel was very surprised by this remark, but he did not interrupt his host.

"I and my team and the police spent days sifting through the ashes but we never found anything," Andrew went on.

"So what was it that made it dodgy?"

"The fire started at about three o'clock in the morning. It was thought to have been started by a lump of hot coal falling onto the carpet in the dining room. Mr Schneider was found outside the front door, which was unlocked. He had apparently died from smoke inhalation."

"What, outside the building? Is that possible?"

"Yes, It's possible but unlikely. You see the seat of the fire was at the back of the building and he was found at the front. The other strange thing is that the dining room was the only room to have a coal fire lit. None of the other rooms, including the lounge, even had a fire laid. Which is not surprising, when you consider it was August and the dining room was hardly ever used."

"You're not saying it was done deliberately, are you?"

"No, I'm not saying anything really. I submitted my concerns in a report along with the police and that was the end of that. The post mortem was unclear by all accounts and the coroner eventually returned a verdict of accidental death, but the insurance company for some reason or another didn't like it and wouldn't pay out. Even so, you'd have thought that the Winterbourne family with all their financial and political muscle would have sorted it by now."

"That's amazing. I never knew any of this and I'm the vicar in charge, or supposed to be, and what about Ethel s husband? What was he doing there?"

Andrew shrugged. "Nobody knew. Not even his ever-loving wife," he said sarcastically.

"I get the impression that you didn't like the Schneiders very much."

"Or the vicar for that matter," replied Andrew. "I've never been much of a churchgoer myself. My wife always went, and I suppose I went along for her sake more than anything else." He cupped his brandy glass in his hands. "There was something about him. He was very impatient with some the older members of his congregation, which is a bit silly really because around here this place is known as god's waiting room, but in other ways he was very generous. The summer outings for the kids for example, he organised the lunch club for the pensioners."

"He didn't pay for that out of the Sunday collections?" interrupted Daniel.

"No, his brother paid for it. The Winterbournes are landed gentry, don't you know. The family seat is somewhere in Norfolk. I think they regarded your predecessor as the runt of the family."

"What makes you say that, apart from the fact you didn't like him?"

"Well, his brother is Henry Winterbourne, the MP and former Home Secretary, for a start."

"Well if they've got all this money, why don't they rebuild the bloody vicarage then? Whoops, there I go again."

"You're not like ordinary vicars, are you Dan?"

"I'm sorry! It's becoming a habit."

Daniel rose from his chair and shook Andrew's hand. "I do hope we can meet again, and I don't mean in church either. Like you, I sometimes wonder if I am in the right job."

"What I said before was meant as a compliment. In fact it's a pleasant surprise to find a human being wearing a dog collar."

Daniel was halfway down the drive when he stopped and turned to Andrew, who was standing in the porch.

Something was bothering him, and he wasn't sure what.

"What was the name of that boy?"

"Stephen, Stephen Jennings."

Something stirred in Daniel's memory. Those initials – SJ.

Chapter 10

The lounge bar of the Olde Kings Head was full to overflowing when Malcolm Cammock and Norman Harris arrived. They made their way slowly through the crowd towards Chief Superintendent Wilkes and the others, who were standing at the far end of the bar.

"Two pints please Tom," said Malcolm over the heads of those in front of him.

Tom placed the order on the bar as they reached the others. "On the house guv, hope you get the bastard," he said.

"Cheers Tom. It won't be for the want of trying."

"Any clues yet, Chief Superintendent?" said an eager voice from a group of reporters who were standing nearby.

Wilkes didn't bother to turn round. He knew it would be the press and he didn't have a lot of time for them, especially when he was relaxing with his team.

"You won't find too many murderers in here," said a rather drunken young reporter. "Shouldn't you be out there trying to catch them instead of pissing it up in here?"

Before anyone could respond, Tom flung back the bar hatch. It crashed against the wooden surface and all the patrons in the bar fell silent. As all the regulars knew, Tom was not a man to be trifled with. He stood face to face with the young reporter, who was probably forty years his junior.

"This is my drink," he said, removing the half empty pint glass from the man's grasp. "My carpet, my chair and my home, so get your feet off my carpet, your bum off my chair and get out."

There was never any point in arguing with Tom, especially when he was backed up by likes of Vincent Bradley and other regulars. You just went quietly, if you had any sense.

The group of reporters downed the remains of their drinks and left quietly. Most of them apologised to Tom and Chief Superintendent Wilkes as they left. Tom acknowledged their apology with a nod of his head. They would be allowed back into his pub, but the boy who had offended him would have no chance as long as he was around.

Tom returned to his rightful place behind the bar and carried on as though nothing had happened. Nobody noticed him replace Vincent Bradley's empty glass with a full one, and if they did, they weren't going to mention it. It was just Tom's way of saying thank you. No words were exchanged.

The rest of the team arrived soon after. It wasn't the done thing to arrive at the pub before the boss. It was very often at times like this, when the team were relaxing, that new ideas were more forthcoming. One such suggestion came from Alan Shaw, the youngest member of the team.

"Sir, I know we are looking at the murders of children, but what about those where the child is just listed as missing? They wouldn't be listed as murders, just missing. You know, no body has ever been found, that sort of thing."

Norman Harris, who was standing with them, grinned.

"Don't look at me boss. Did you think of it?"

"First thing tomorrow Norman, I want you to go up the yard and get all the info on missing children. Boys and girls aged between twelve and eighteen who have been missing for more than a year in London and the surrounding areas."

"Does that mean we can skip the trip to the post mortem?" said Norman, his grin getting even broader.

"No it doesn't. You can do this afterwards," replied Inspector Cammock. "But Alan can buy the next round for embarrassing you."

Chapter 11

"That was a lovely meal, Dan. Housekeeper *and* cook, now that is exceptional," said June, after finishing off the last of the cheesecake.

"All in a day's work for your average vicar," replied Dan as he poured the last of the wine.

The evening had been a great success. June and Dan had talked all through dinner, which had been simple fare but very appetising. June had talked about her life in the village and about Derek's disappearance, but this time without so much emotion. Daniel had talked about his army career and how his Christian beliefs had been stretched to the limit over what he had seen.

"I felt so sorry for the parents of that boy they found

today, but it's something you said earlier," he said. "At least they will be able to bury him and say their goodbyes, but you, you must be in limbo not knowing if he's actually dead or alive."

"You're right Dan. That's why I stay in the village. I know in my heart of hearts that he's dead, but there is always the chance, no matter how remote, that one day he might return, and if that ever happens I want to be here."

Daniel poured some coffee. "Shall we go through to the lounge? I'm afraid that's the last of the good wine, unless you fancy some of Mrs Saunders' home-made carrot wine."

They both stood and made their way to the lounge where the coal fire was still smouldering.

"No thanks, I've seen what it's done to her husband. A brandy will do nicely."

"I'm sorry, if my congregation don't supply it, I don't have it."

"You don't fancy a stroll to the pub do you? It's only just round the corner. Do you know the one I mean?" said June.

"Yes" replied Daniel." I've been in there once or twice."

"That's great! On one condition though, I buy the drinks. You're not one of these men who won't let the weaker sex buy a drink are you?"

"Believe me, we vicars will accept charity from any quarter, even bossy lady reporters."

They laughed, something they had been doing most of the evening, and it felt good. They walked arm in arm down the lane that would take them past the old tower. As they got closer, Daniel suddenly stopped.

"I've got it!" he said. "Why didn't I think of it sooner?"

June stopped, startled. "What are you talking about? You just frightened the life out of me!"

"I'm sorry, something's been bothering me and I just couldn't put my finger on it. On the morning of the funeral, I came round this way past the old tower." Daniel pointed through the darkness at the tower that stood silhouetted against the night sky.

June started to laugh. "You're just trying to frighten me." She gave his arm a playful punch. "Nobody goes in there."

"No honestly June, I'm being serious. I found a small black wallet with the initials S.J. in gold lettering. I didn't think much of it at the time, only that they are the same initials as that poor boy who was murdered, Stephen Jennings"

"Now you are beginning to frighten me. You must tell the police at once. It's too much of a coincidence."

"I also found a porn mag, that's why I didn't take much notice. I thought it was a few boys from the village."

"You're joking! Nobody ever goes in there. When I was a kid we always went the long way round just to avoid it."

"Oh, you mean the sound of bells ringing in the night and the sounds of screaming from the tower." Daniel spoke as if he was a cross between the Hunchback of Notre Dame and Boris Karloff. She laughed at his poor joke and again pushed him away, but this time he held on to her. It was a simple act of intimacy that only people getting to know each other fully understand.

"I'm being serious. If you're right it might mean that Stephen was here, actually in the graveyard. Have you told the police?"

"Sort of."

June looked bemused.

"I invited Vince Bradley back to the cottage after the funeral and we had rather a lot to drink. I remember telling him about it and he must have taken them with him. The problem is, will he remember?"

They continued their short walk and soon reached the pub. Daniel pushed open the saloon door and ushered June in. He knew that his being with June was going to start a few rumours, but he didn't mind. He acknowledged welcomes from several people who knew him. June eased her way to the front of the bar.

"Evening June, evening Daniel," said Tom with a silly smile on his face. He certainly wasn't going to say anything – or was he? Either way, you knew exactly what he was thinking.

"Two large brandies please Tom," said June.

"Out with father tonight?" said Tom, letting out a snort of laughter. "I'm sorry, I couldn't resist it."

They picked up their drinks and made their way to one end of the bar. Almost at once Daniel thought he recognised someone, but it couldn't be, he thought. The last time he had seen that man had been in Northern Ireland.

"Is that someone you know?" said June, seeing him staring. But he was already making his way towards a group of men.

"Malcolm?" said Daniel. "Malcolm Cammock?"

His companions turned to face the newcomer in their midst. Malcolm could hardly believe his eyes, his instant recognition beaming all over his face. The two men embraced each other warmly.

"You old bugger," said Malcolm. "What are you doing here? Are you still..."

Daniel pulled down the top of his sweater to reveal his clerical collar. "I work here. I'm at St. Andrew's, here in the village. But what about you?"

"I'm a DI. I'm on the squad investigating that boy's murder." Malcolm started to introduce his old friend to the squad. "Sir, you're not going to believe this but the last time I saw this man I had been hiding in a ditch for twelve hours after my car broke down in bandit country and Dan here turned up with his mates and saved my arse."

Daniel shook everyone's hands.

"So you've only got me to blame," said Daniel jokingly. "And those days are best forgotten. Let me introduce you to June here."

"Yes, I saw you this morning at the banqueting hall," said Wilkes to June. "Thanks for the photographs by the way, they came out well." His words were like a coded warning to his troops: "Enemy in the camp. Don't discuss the job."

"Well I've got to go. See you all in the morning. Good night Miss Walsh, and you, vicar."

The Chief Superintendent left the pub with the rest of the team. Malcolm, Norman and Alan stayed behind.

"Don't mind him June, he's had a long day," Malcolm.

"That's quite all right. I made a complete fool of myself, I'm sorry."

"I know you can't discuss your investigation, Malcolm, but did you get the wallet I found belonging to Stephen Jennings?" asked Daniel. "Or at least I think it's his."

Malcolm looked at Norman, who shrugged and shook his head. "I haven't got the remotest idea what you're talking about, Daniel."

Daniel recounted the story of when and how he had

found the wallet. "I remember it had the initials SJ on it. I gave it to Vincent Bradley after the funeral service."

"He was here just a minute ago," said Alan.

"Yes, that was a funny old business. We've never had anything like that before."

"Do you think they are linked?" enquired June.

Daniel realised that Malcolm and Norman felt uncomfortable about discussing anything to do with the case in front of June, who was after all a reporter.

"It's all right, June knows all about this and she has her own reasons for helping you," he said. "But I'll let her tell you about that herself. You can trust her, believe me."

"Time gentlemen please!" called Tom from the bar.

"Has Vincent Bradley gone, Tom?" asked Malcolm.

"Just walked out the door."

"Alan, you know where he lives, chase after him and get that wallet."

Alan was nearly out of the door when Daniel shouted after him, "Don't forget the porn magazine as well."

The pub fell quiet for a moment and everyone stared in Daniel's direction.

"Oh dear, sorry. Look, why not come back for coffee and on the way I'll show you where I found the wallet and June can tell you about her brother, it may be useful," Daniel said to Malcolm.

"What's this about a porn magazine?"

"I found that at the same time. They weren't together

or anything."

Outside the pub, Alan came running back towards them. "I've got them," he said breathlessly. "They were still in his pocket."

"Right, make sure they are bagged up properly and then take the wallet to Mr and Mrs Jennings first thing in the morning, see if they can identify it," said Malcolm. "If they do, ring me on my mobile. Whatever you do don't show them the magazine. We don't want to upset them any more than they are already."

On the walk back to the cottage via the church tower, June told her story of her brother Derek, how it had affected her family and why she had been so upset at what she saw at the banqueting hall that morning.

"No wonder you were upset. It must have brought back terrible memories," said Malcolm.

"It must have been really shocking for you," said Norman sympathetically.

They came to the narrow path that led through the old graveyard to the tower and peered through the darkness at the outline of the tower against the night sky.

"I found it near the railings over there. You can't see from here and it's too dark anyway," said Daniel quietly, as if he didn't want anyone else to hear.

"What about the magazine? Where was that?"

"It was just off the path, this side of the railings."

"I suppose dozens of people will have walked through here since then," said Norman.

"Oh no, that's just it. Nobody ever comes here. It's too spooky," said June, only too pleased to help.

"June's right. I thought I was the only person to walk through here. The place is supposed to be haunted, you know."

"I'm not surprised. This place gives me the creeps, and we're still standing in the road," said Norman, walking off. "And besides, we don't even know if the wallet was Stephen's yet."

No sooner had Norman stopped speaking than Malcolm's mobile phone burst into life, making everybody jump. It sounded even more eerie as they were standing at the edge of a graveyard.

"Jesus! Sorry everyone," said Norman, patting his heart as though to keep it going.

"Well done Alan! See you in the morning. He's a good officer that Alan," said Malcolm.

"What's he done now?" asked Norman.

"He drove passed the Jennings' house, and the light was on so he knocked. They have positively identified the wallet as belonging to Stephen."

"Are you saying he could have been murdered here in, my churchyard?"

"We don't know. It could have been dropped by anyone at any time. We'll need to go over this area with a fine-tooth comb. I want some uniform here all night if necessary, or at least until the forensic turn up. Will you organise that, Norman?"

"Do you think they might come back?" asked June nervously.

"I just don't know June, but anything is possible."

June gripped Daniel's hand tighter. For a moment he thought she was going to cry. Daniel sensed her unease and placed his arm around her shoulder.

"It's a very large area to cover guv. I'm just wondering if a dog handler might be better," said Norman.

"Do what you think best Norman. I just want forensics, photographic and a search team here first thing in the morning. That reminds me, Daniel. Do you have a key to the church tower?"

Chapter 12

Daniel rose early the next morning. He showered and dressed quickly in his usual jeans with a sweater pulled over his clerical collar. He was in the kitchen making some fresh coffee when he heard a car pull onto his gravel drive. He looked at his watch; It was still only 6.30. He went to the window and was surprised to see Malcolm and Norman climbing out of a car. He watched them as they went over to look at his Hillman Minx. He opened the front door quietly and listened to what they were saying.

"I'm surprised it's taxed. The tax is worth more than the car, if you ask me. Mark you, it looks solid enough" replied Norman, gently banging the roof of the car.

"You two aren't being rude about my car, are you?" said Daniel.

"You don't actually drive this on the roads, do you?" said Malcolm, shaking his old friend by the hand.

"What are you doing here at this time of the morning, can't you sleep?" replied Daniel.

Both men followed Daniel through to the kitchen, where the smell of fresh coffee permeated the air. The two men seated themselves around the table and Daniel realised that his last comment might not be far from the truth.

"Have you two been up all night, or do you normally wear the same clothes two days running?" asked Daniel.

"You should have been a detective."

It was obvious by the sarcasm in Malcolm's voice that he was both tired and annoyed.

Daniel handed each of them a mug of coffee. "Has something happened? Has there been a development?" he asked.

"You could say that," said Malcolm, taking a sip of coffee. "Someone went and tipped off the press about what we are doing this morning. The guvnor here has been fending off questions all night from the press. Even the big house have been on."

"Big house?" queried Daniel.

"Scotland Yard, Dan. They want to know why I'm about to dig up a graveyard. It's a real media scrum out there, thanks to someone."

"Well who would have told them?"

"I think we all know the answer to that one, Dan,"

said Norman.

"If you mean Ju..."

Before Daniel could finish, June was standing at the kitchen door, wearing Daniel's dressing gown.

"Actually Inspector, I've got an alibi," she said. She walked into the room and kissed Daniel gently on the cheek. "Have we got eggs and bacon, darling?" she said, blushing slightly.

Malcolm and Norman rose from their seats, feeling a little embarrassed at what they had said, and June kissed each of them on the cheek. Malcolm was about to say something when she raised her hand as if to silence him.

"Don't apologise. I'm on your side, remember. Now how do you like your eggs?"

"I am delighted to confirm June's alibi" said Stan and gave her a hug.

"Look, I'm sorry June. We've been up all night and..."

"I said don't apologise. Now don't give it another thought, and for the last time, how do you like your eggs?"

"With other eggs," said Norman. "I'm starving."

"I think I've found the key to the tower" said Daniel, laying a bunch of keys on the table.

"What do you mean, you think? Have you never been inside?"

"Good heavens no, nor has anyone else to my knowledge, it's been locked up for years. If there was a problem I would just call the Bishop's office and they would deal with it. I've certainly had no reason to go in there."

"So it's going to be a first time for us all," said Malcolm. "Let's hope we've got the right key. With the press outside, I would like things to go smoothly."

"You mean you don't want to look a prat in front of them," said Norman with a grin on his face.

"I was trying to be polite in front of our host."

"You, diplomatic? You're about as diplomatic as a flying house brick!" laughed Norman.

The four of them settled down to a fried feast, with coffee and toast which June had prepared for them. Then Norman went into the hall to phone his wife and freshen up before starting another long day.

"Malcolm, if you want to ring Alice, feel free to use the phone," said Dan. "How is she? It's been years."

"Actually Dan, we're separated, quite recently in fact."

Daniel was genuinely shocked. They had always seemed the perfect army couple.

"I always thought you were so happy. I thought when you left the army, you would settle down, perhaps start a family."

" We've got two boys. Unfortunately, this job is worse than the army. You've seen what it's like. Actually Dan, if it's all the same to you, I'd rather keep my mind on the job in hand."

"I'm sorry. It's not my place to tell you how to run your life, but if I can help in any way…"

"I thought wearing that dog collar – sorry, clerical collar – gave you every right," said Norman as he entered the room, drying his hair with a towel.

Malcolm felt very uncomfortable discussing his private life. It was June who came to his rescue and changed the subject. "Have you told anyone else to come here? Only there's half the police force outside."

"Oh God! Dan. I'm sorry. I meant to ask you before, do you mind if we use this place as a base? We won't be trampling over everything. It's just that I need to brief the troops when they arrive."

At that point the doorbell rang and June went to answer it. Daniel could see Malcolm's unease at being questioned about his private life. "No problem, anything I can do to help, you only have to ask," he said.

"Thanks mate," Malcolm replied as he disappeared out of the door. Norman followed him out, but before he left he turned to Daniel and said, "They both want their heads banging together, if you ask me."

"He didn't ask you!" Malcolm called out from the hall.

"See what I mean, very touchy" replied Norman and followed his boss into the hall. Almost immediately they returned.

"OK Daniel, let's go, and don't forget the keys."

"What do you want me for?"

"Well, it's your tower, and besides I need you to show me exactly where you found that wallet."

Malcolm turned to June. "I'm sorry June, we can't let you come with us. You do understand, don't you? It's not that I don't trust you, it's just that the rest of the press will want to know why you've being given preferential treatment."

"Don't worry, of course I understand, but promise me one thing."

"What's that?"

"If your investigation turns up anything about Derek, I want to know straight away."

"That's a promise."

The three men made their way down the lane towards the old tower. In the distance they could see a large group of reporters and several others carrying video cameras. The journalists were herded behind a police tape, but when they saw the three men approaching several of them broke away and ran towards them.

"Can you tell us exactly what you're going to do Inspector?" said a young reporter with a smug look on his face who was strangely familiar. He was hoping that with the television cameras there, Inspector Cammock would be more forthcoming.

"Yes, certainly."

Just for a moment Norman was staggered that his boss was even going to acknowledge the young reporter's presence, let alone speak to him. Immediately a crowd of reporters gathered round, eager for a story. Malcolm looked the young pressman straight in the eyes.

"Your behaviour last night was disgusting. You belong to an honourable profession, but your drunken, loutish behaviour..."

"CUT!" said a voice from the crowd, and roars of laughter rose from the rest.

"Nice one Mr Cammock. Have you got a comment for one of your old reliable drunks?" said one of the older reporters.

"Hello Jimmy." The two men shook hands.

"There really isn't much to tell," said Malcolm. "There's a slim chance that the boy who was found at the banqueting hall site yesterday may have passed through this churchyard. I honestly don't expect to find anything, but if you want to hang around you're more than welcome."

"We understood you were about to dig up several graves."

"I don't know who started these stupid rumours, but if I find out, they will be in serious sh... er, trouble."

"Why are the forensic boys here then?" said another reporter.

"It's just standard procedure."

"Is there any connection between the boy's murder and the graves that were desecrated?"

"As far as we can tell, there is no connection at all. Now you must excuse me. I really want to get this over and done with as quickly as possible. If you want to hang around you're more than welcome, but please keep your distance."

Malcolm, Norman and Daniel started up the path towards the tower, where a young police officer was standing.

"Sorry about this son, you'll be off home in half an hour," said Malcolm, in a voice just loud enough to be heard by the majority of the reporters. They continued along the path and Malcolm glanced round and smiled when he saw several of the press corps starting to leave, which was what he wanted.

"It's very overgrown in here. How do you know who's buried where?" he asked Daniel. "I mean some of these graves have nearly disappeared altogether."

"We have records dating back to the sixteenth century."

"Here, look at this one," said Norman. "This fella was blown up in the Gunpowder Mill. So was this one. I didn't even know we had a mill."

"It's over by the stream on the other side of the village. It's been turned into smart offices now. I find old graveyards fascinating, full of history."

"Somebody else thinks so too. Some of these stones have been re-engraved," said Malcolm.

"Yes, I noticed that yesterday," said Daniel as the trio made their way along the path towards the tower. "Perhaps there's some sort of historical society in Etwell, but I've never heard of one."

They reached the railings and the iron gate that had protected the tower for the past 150 years. It was padlocked with a heavy chain wrapped around ironwork. Daniel tried all his keys one by one in the lock.

"I don't seem to have one that fits this lock."

"Hold up a minute Dan, is it my imagination or does this lock seem new to you?" said Malcolm.

Both Malcolm and Norman examined the lock.

"You're right guv, it looks quite new to me," said Norman.

Malcolm's attention became focused. "Show me exactly where you found the wallet, Dan."

Daniel pointed to a spot to the right of the gate. "It was about here," he said. "Or it may have been a bit further in, I'm not sure."

"I'm not happy about this Norman. Let's have the Soco up here to cut this lock off and bag it and then we'll have the search team to go over this area around the tower before we go in."

"We're not even sure the boy was here," said Norman.

"But the wallet was identified by his parents," replied Daniel.

"Yes, but that doesn't mean he was here. He could

have lost it somewhere else and whoever found it threw it in here."

"Yes, I see what you mean Malcolm. Well, you know what you're doing."

Norman had already gone to get the search team who were waiting near the cottage. Daniel stood back and watched as the team began their search of the area. A man who Daniel guessed was the scenes of crime officer cut the padlock from the chain. The man wore thin latex gloves. He examined the lock and chain carefully and placed them in a bag.

"That's this area clear now, guv," said a man wearing blue overalls. Daniel noticed the sergeant's insignia on his shoulder.

"We haven't found much of interest, only a large amount of guano."

"What's that?" said Norman inquisitively.

"Bird shit to you," replied Malcolm. "OK Daniel. Do your stuff and unlock the door."

"Shouldn't you be doing this? After all, you're in charge."

"No, that's all right Dan. It's your church. If there is anyone in there, they won't hurt you, you being a vicar an' all." Norman smiled at his boss.

"Thanks very much," said Daniel sarcastically. He walked through the open iron gate towards the large oak door that led into the tower itself. Its age belied its strength. Daniel pushed the large key effortlessly into the lock and turned it.

"I thought it would have been rusted through," said Daniel to the other two, who were crowding just behind him.

"Hmm... see if it will open," said Malcolm.

Daniel pushed against the door, but it stood firm.

"Give it a good shove," said Norman.

Daniel put his shoulder to the door again and this time, with one good shove, it moved slowly back. The door swung silently back and came to rest against an old pew which had been stood on its end behind it.

"After you Inspector," said Malcolm.

Daniel stood back and ushered his friend inside. Norman followed his boss into the tower. Although it was daylight outside, the thick vegetation surrounding the tower made it very dark inside.

"Bring me a light, somebody," said Norman. A member of the search team who was standing outside brought in a flashlight and handed it to him.

The floor was made of solid stone slabs. It seemed much larger inside than it did from the outside; about twenty feet square. Furthest from the door was a wooden platform, and from one side of this a wooden staircase rose about twenty feet to another platform. From that another flight of wooden steps rose up to a trap door in a wooden floor high above their heads. Up in the rafters, dozens of jackdaws protested noisily at being disturbed as Norman shone the torch slowly around the floor.

Daniel wondered if the other two were as relieved as he was that there were no dead bodies to be seen. There was only a pile of broken headstones.

"This place is really open to the elements," said Norman. "That roof can't be too strong.

"I suppose that must be bird droppings I can smell," said Norman, sniffing the air.

Malcolm and Daniel followed his example.

"That's not bird shit, that's polish. You know, furniture polish," said Malcolm.

He swung the torch around the room once again. Alongside the pew that was standing upright behind the door was another pew. This one, however, was leant up against the wall and covered by an old woollen blanket. Malcolm pulled off the cover. Underneath they could see a smooth polished surface.

"I don't understand," said Malcolm. "Why would somebody polish a broken pew that nobody is ever going to sit on?"

"This is bloody weird, guv." Norman took the torch out of Malcolm's hand and shone it round the tower once more. Its beam came to rest on an old stone cross that was leaning against the wall. It was about five feet high and very thick.

"Oh God!"

"What is it? What have you found?"

The three men stood transfixed by the beam of light that played over the stone cross. At either side of the cross were wide leather straps and buckles, and at the base of the cross was a wider strap and buckle. Norman stepped forward slowly to examine the stone cross, careful not to disturb anything. He bent down to get a closer look at the base of the cross.

"It's blood, governor. It's all over the place."

"Right, let's get outside," said Malcolm quietly. He saw the look on Daniel's face and gripped his arm.

"Are you all right, Dan?"

"No, I'm bloody not all right," replied Daniel quietly. He realised that their discovery was not to be shared with others, but that did not make him any the less angry.

"That boy was crucified! In my church!" he snarled.

Once outside they stood and breathed in the fresh air.

"OK. We are probably being photographed as we speak, so don't give too much away," said Malcolm authoritatively. "Norman, I want this place sealed off. I don't want anybody coming into this cemetery. Get the forensic boys in here straight away. I want it gone over from top to bottom." He looked to the top of the tower. "And I do mean top to bottom."

Norman nodded his acknowledgment. He was about to leave when Malcolm grabbed his arm. "We must keep the lid on this. I'll be at Dan's place. Is that OK with you Dan? We'll wait here until you come back."

Norman returned almost immediately with several men, who started to put on white overalls and fit plastic bags over their feet. High-powered arc lights were placed in position. Malcolm quietly briefed his men. Norman also changed into forensic clothing.

"Take your time, Norman. Call me If you find anything, anything at all," said Malcolm.

Norman stood back and let the experts into the tower. He watched his boss leaving via the new church to avoid any pressmen that might be remaining.

"You'll have to get someone else to do the post mortem," Norman called after his boss.

Chapter 13

Malcolm and Daniel made their way back to the cottage via the war memorial and along the path that led through the new church cemetery, past the grave of Mrs Schneider with all its fresh flowers laid out either side. Traces of red paint were still visible on the headstones and the wall behind.

"Do you don't think these two incidents are connected?" said Daniel as they strolled purposefully along. "I mean nothing ever happens in Etwell, and now this."

"I honestly don't know, but whoever did that in the tower has got to be a right sick evil bastard. How do you do that sort of thing?"

They continued the rest of the short journey to the vicarage in silence.

"I don't want June told anything about this Dan, not at the moment anyway."

"Don't worry, I agree with you. There's no point in upsetting her any more than she is already."

They entered the vicarage and walked through to the kitchen. Daniel called out to June and was relieved when she didn't answer.

"She's probably gone back to her own place, or to work," he said. Either way it meant that he wouldn't have to lie to her or pretend everything was all right.

Malcolm spent some time on the phone to the office issuing instructions. "Any problems, you can contact me here on this number. No, I'll notify Mr Wilkes, and remember I want this kept quiet for now."

He replaced the receiver and went through to the kitchen to join Daniel, who had already poured the coffee into mugs and was seated at the table.

"How long will your forensic chaps be?" asked Daniel. "Not that there's any rush on my part."

"Thanks Dan. I don't know. It's up to the guys in that tower now, they're the experts. Let's hope they can come up with something so we can nail this bastard."

Malcolm drank his coffee and was busy writing notes in a small book.

"Changing the subject," said Daniel, but what has happened between you and Alice? I mean you were so close. And don't tell me it's none of my business, I've known you too long for that."

Malcolm stopped writing and looked at his friend. He realised that Daniel was not going to be fobbed off.

"Alice was so looking forward to me leaving the army." Malcolm paused for a moment, as though reflecting on his past life. "She has put up with a lot from me. We've lived all over the world. Some postings were good, but most of them were bloody awful, but she never complained once. I was reluctant to leave the army at first, but with the pension I was going to be better off than most and I was determined to put Alice and the kids first for a change."

"What happened?"

"I joined this job, that's what happened. I love it, but instead of being thousands of miles apart, you know active service, now I'm just down the road, but I might just as well be on the moon. I never saw it coming, I didn't see the signs. She never said anything, and if she did I wasn't listening. I was too busy playing policeman."

"I don't understand. What signs?"

"The signs that should have told me that she was having an affair."

"You're joking. I don't believe it! Not Alice. She's the last person, and she loved you so much. Anyone who knew you both could see that."

"I ignored her for too long. I was too busy wrapped up in the job. Then over the weekend I found out purely by chance that she had been seeing someone else."

"Who is this fella? Do you know him?"

Malcolm half smiled. "Yes, I know him all right."

"Where is she now?" asked Daniel, refilling their mugs with coffee.

"She's in the house with the kids. We had a blazing row and I left the same day."

"But she's not seeing him now?"

"What do you mean?"

"You said she had an affair, which implies that it's over."

"You don't understand Daniel. I mean this guy was one of my uniformed PCs."

"Oh! so it's your pride that's hurt. Are you going to throw away all those years of marriage because she made a mistake? Did she want you to go?"

"No."

"Well then."

"It's all too late now. You can't turn back the clock."

"It's never too late, and it's obvious from the way you're talking that you still love her."

Malcolm fell silent and drank his coffee. Daniel started making some more.

"You know, it's the little things I miss. Just sitting down and talking about my day, I suppose that was it really. I always told her what I was doing. I never asked her what she or the children were doing. I never showed any interest, but you're right, I still love her and the children, I miss them."

"Where are you living now?"

"I'm in a bedsit in Woking at the moment."

"What! Are you travelling all that way every day? Why don't you come and live here until things are sorted out? Or better still, go home and make it up with Alice."

"I can't do that. Anyway, what about June? She might have something to say about me staying here."

"Don't be daft, we're not engaged or anything like that and besides I've got a spare room."

"She's a lovely lady," grinned Malcolm.

"We only met a few days ago," protested Daniel.

"You don't have to convince me, Dan. If you're sure you don't mind, I would love to take you up on your offer."

"That's settled then. Come on, I'll show you your room."

Chapter 14

Arc lights had been brought in to illuminate the dark tower. Norman stood silently watching the forensic officers scrape samples of blood from the stone cross. After examination, the leather buckles and straps were carefully removed and bagged up.

They had decided to start on one side of the tower and work round the floor together, as this way they hoped they would disturb as little as possible. It was a long process, but inch by inch they completed the search on their hands and knees. The polished bench was examined thoroughly. The remains of fingerprint officers' silver dust covered the entire bench. The sheet that had covered it was carefully folded and it too was bagged up for closer examination back at the laboratory. The upright bench behind the door was lowered and examined in the same thorough manner.

The forensic officers finished their examination of the floor area and two of them were now painstakingly examining each step of the staircase in turn, slowly making their way up the tower.

"You lads be careful, I don't want those stairs collapsing on me," called Norman to the two men, who were by now about half way up.

"Thanks for your concern Norm. In fact it's quite safe. These stairs have been replaced in the past hundred years or so. They'll be good for another hundred."

"Can you open the trap door and get out onto the tower?" called one of the men.

A man climbed up the staircase to the top and examined the lock for what seemed a long time.

"Well?" called the man.

"This lock hasn't been open for years. It's completely rusted through," shouted the man. At that, the jackdaws that had so far been silent at the intrusion into their home flew around his head, chack-chacking their annoyance and forcing him to beat a hasty retreat to the ground floor.

"I want the door opened if that's OK with you," said Norman. "I just want to be sure there's nothing up there."

"No problem," said the man who was obviously in charge of the forensic team. He smiled at the one who had just come down.

"Thanks," said the man. He delved into bag and produced a hammer and chisel.

"Have we found anything, anything at all?" asked Norman, already half knowing what the reply would be.

"Nothing. unless we get something off the sheet or the buckles at the lab. There's a few finger marks but nothing more. I'm almost certain they wore gloves."

"When you say 'they', do you know there was more than one?"

"Again I won't be sure until we get to the lab, but I'm pretty sure that at least two people sat on this bench. I think we've found three sets of footprints. One is obviously a pair of trainers that possibly belonged to the boy, which will be easy to check."

"Why would someone polish a bench?" said Norman.

"Look, I don't know for certain, but the position of the bench and the footprints in relation to the cross suggest that while one of them was abusing the boy the other person or persons sat on the bench and watched."

"What sort of people are we dealing with? They must be fucking sick!" Norman was disgusted at the thought.

"Has anyone looked at this?" said one of the men, pointing to a metal plate fixed on the wall about six feet up. It measured about nine inches square and had four bolts securing it to the wall.

"What is it?" asked Norman inquisitively.

"It looks like one of those old gas covers. You know,

in the old days when they had gas lighting."

"This place hasn't been used for a hundred and fifty years," said one of the men.

"Did they have gas lighting in those days?" asked another.

"I don't know, but see what's behind it anyway," said Norman.

One of the men produced an adjustable spanner and started to undo the bolts at each corner of the plate. The first bolt turned easily and the man stopped what he was doing.

"I think we should dust this first. These bolts are only finger tight. I think this plate has been removed recently."

They gathered round as a man brushed lightly over the plate with his brush.

"Nothing here," said the man, shaking his head.

"Let me do that," said Norman. He stepped forward and started undoing the bolts. One by one they dropped into his hand. Nobody spoke, and there was no sound but their breathing and the occasional bird screeching high above them.

Norman gently removed the metal plate from the wall and handed it to someone else, who carefully placed it in a bag. The space behind the plate was about 12 inches deep, and Norman placed his hand inside and drew out a white plastic bag. It had been folded over several times and stuck down with Sellotape to protect its contents. Norman placed the bag on a small table and one of the forensic scientists came forward and carefully slit the side of the bag with a razor. He then tipped the contents onto the table.

"I don't bloody believe this."

"Oh Jesus Christ!"

"What the fucking hell's going on?"

One after another the men voiced their disgust, as one by one the Polaroid photographs were placed on the table before them. They were all of naked boys, and several of them showed in graphic detail Stephen Jennings strapped to the stone cross and a man, his face hidden from view, kissing his genitalia. Another showed another naked boy, his eyes wide with fear, a penis held against his face and a large hand on his shoulder.

"Those poor bastards," said Norman, staring at the obscenities in front of him. He paused for a moment, as if to fully take in what his eyes were looking at.

"OK, get them dusted and bagged. I don't want anyone talking about this until we know what we're dealing with. Let's make quite sure we haven't missed anything." Norman reached for his mobile phone. "Hello guv, Is that you? You'd better come down and have a look at this. And bring Dan along with you." Norman paused for a moment. "We've found some photographs guv. They're bloody awful."

Malcolm and Daniel retraced their steps back to the tower. When they arrived, Norman was waiting outside for them. His face was pale and drawn.

"It's photographs of kids," said Norman, trying to subdue the enormous emotion he felt inside.

"Why did you want Daniel to come along?"

"I thought if they're local kids he might recognise some of them, and I thought the fewer people that know about this the better," replied Norman.

"How do you feel about that, Dan?" said Malcolm.

"I've got to warn you they are pretty horrific," interrupted Norman.

"I've never dealt with anything like this before, but if I can help..." Daniel shrugged in unwilling compliance.

"I don't think many people have. Let's get on with it," said Malcolm.

The three men entered the tower. The photographs were laid out on the table in individual transparent bags.

"There are twenty-three photos in all sir," said the senior forensic officer. "As far as I can tell they are all of different boys, but I can't be sure about that. Their ages seem to range from about ten to fourteen years. Again I'll be able to give you a more accurate date when we've got them back to the lab. As for the content, see for yourself."

The man stepped back from the table, enabling the

three men to see more closely.

Daniel cupped his hand over his mouth when he saw the photographs. He felt the bile deep in his throat start to rise, and it was all he could do to stop himself from being sick.

The three men stood there taking the full horror of what lay in front of them.

"They're just children!" exclaimed Daniel, scarcely believing what he was looking at.

"Do you recognise any of them Dan?" said Malcolm, placing a hand on his shoulder.

"No I don't, thank god. I've seen enough. I'll wait outside if you don't mind." Daniel started to make his way outside.

"There's just one other thing, sir," said the senior forensic scientist. "These photographs appear to have been taken over a long period of time."

"What do you mean?" snapped Malcolm, annoyed at the man's apparent lack of feeling.

"Well, If you look carefully you can see that some of them are beginning to fade. I rather fancy that they are several years old. I will be able to give you a better idea..."

"Yes I know, when you get back to the lab. Just give me your informed opinion," said Malcolm.

"I would say that some of them are at least ten to fifteen years old. This one, for example." He pointed to one of the photographs. "The print itself was taken on one of the early Instamatic cameras. And before you say anything else, Inspector, I would like to add that I am also a father of two young boys. I can assure you sir that my team will be working flat out to get the results you want."

"I'm sorry, this is upsetting for all of us. How many copies can I have and how soon, and what is your name?"

"Digweed, sir. Jack Digweed. You'll have my report by this evening. Will ten copies be enough?"

"That will be enough for the time being. One more thing, I'm sure Norman's already mentioned this but I want this kept under wraps. Is that clear? And thanks Jack."

Malcolm and Norman joined Daniel outside.

"Are you all right Dan?" asked Malcolm.

"I've never seen anything like that in my life before. They were just young boys, children. How can someone do that sort of thing?"

"I don't know, but we have to catch these evil bastards. We need to identify those boys. Are you sure you didn't recognise any of them?"

"I'm quite sure, but if that man is right, I've only been here three years and some of those boys could be grown up and married by now."

"Or dead," replied Norman.

"I suppose you realise that one of those boys could be

June's brother Derek?" said Daniel.

"Yes, I had thought of that," said Malcolm, who was deep in thought.

"We can't just show her all those photographs, it would be too upsetting. Specially if one of them turned out to be her brother."

"I might have an idea. I met a man yesterday, Andrew Summers. It was his grandchildren that found the body of that boy. His wife was a teacher at the village school, but she died last year."

"I'm not sure I know what you're getting at, Dan."

"I'm sorry. I'm not making myself very clear. His wife kept a yearbook of all the students. It's unlikely, but if they are local and they went to the village school then Andrew may have a photograph of one of the boys. Either way he will be able to identify Derek."

"OK Dan. We're going back to the office. When we get all the photographs blown up we'll go round and see your man. See you later."

Daniel made his way back to his cottage. He was wondering if June had returned, and was rather hoping she had not, but as he entered the cottage she appeared holding two mugs of coffee.

"Did they find anything?" she asked.

"Yes they did. I'm not sure what exactly, Malcolm said he would tell me tonight. By the way, Malcolm's moving in for a few days until things have been sorted out," said Daniel, changing the subject.

"That's very nice of you."

Chapter 15

The office meeting had been brought forward by two hours. Chief Superintendent Wilkes was already being brought up to speed on the events of the past few hours by Malcolm, Norman and Claire Billings in a small office adjacent to the main committee room prior to the full squad meeting.

All the team were present when they eventually emerged. There had been much speculation but only a handful knew what exactly had happened. They were about to find out. The room hushed as Chief Superintendent Wilkes got up to speak. He adopted his usual no-nonsense manner, but even he had trouble masking his true feelings.

"Right, ladies and gentlemen. Before Inspector

Cammock briefs you on what's happened this morning, I want to warn you, especially you younger members, that what you're going to see and investigate is without doubt the worst catalogue of depraved acts of indecency against boys I have ever seen in my nearly thirty years of service, and quite frankly I thought I had seen everything. If after this briefing any of you want to withdraw from this squad, I will understand."

The officers shifted uneasily in their seats and looked from one to another.

"Now I'm going to hand you over to Inspector Cammock."

Malcolm rose from his seat. "Before I start I would like to introduce Jack Digweed, who is the senior forensic scientist from the lab. He is going to show you some slides. These slides are copies of photographs found hidden in the old church tower this morning, together with a stone cross about five feet high on which we believe Stephen was murdered. Before he starts I want it clearly understood, and this applies to all of you without exception, that what you see here today must remain within these walls. On no account will any of you discuss what you're about to see outside this office. Is that clear?"

He waited for a moment and looked around the table.

"If anyone would like to leave, now's your chance."

No one moved.

"Right then, first things first. Alan, lock the door. In future that door will be kept locked at all times. I'm having the lock changed and each of you will be given a key. Don't lose it! Will someone draw the curtains? OK Jack, it's all yours."

Jack Digweed stood at one end of the room. The slide projector was already set up and he held the slide switch in his hand.

"Thank you sir. Will someone get the lights? What you are about to see is a series of photographs depicting various acts of indecency and brutality against young boys. These photographs have been taken over a period of about fifteen years. There are twenty-three photographs in all. We're not sure, but we think they show nine different boys. I am going to start with the most recent photograph, which is the only boy we are able to identify, and that is Stephen Jennings, the boy whose body was found yesterday."

Jack Digweed pushed the switch in his hand and the bloodstained body of Stephen Jennings strapped to the stone cross appeared in front of them. The response was instantaneous. Some covered their eyes. Others turned away from the screen, hoping the horror would depart, but it was only just beginning. One by one the photographs were displayed on the screen, and as each example of human depravity was shown the team grew quieter and quieter, until they were stunned into complete silence.

"That's it, lights please," said Jack.

Mr Wilkes, who had been standing in the corner by the light switch, switched them on. Some of his officers were unashamedly wiping tears from their eyes. Others sat with their faces buried in their hands.

"Shall we have some coffee before we go on?" said Wilkes.

Alan Shaw rose from his seat to get the drinks. He wanted to be somewhere else, and making coffee in the kitchen was just the interlude he needed. Coffee and tea were distributed around the table, and slowly the team started to settle down and talk amongst themselves.

"OK. You all now have an idea of what we are dealing with," Malcolm began. "We believe these photographs have been taken over a number of years, and at the moment we only know the identity of one of the boys. Let's have your ideas, and as Mr Wilkes said right at the beginning, it doesn't matter how daft you may think your idea is. We'll soon tell you."

"Have we established that all the photographs were taken in the tower?" said one.

"Can you help with this one?" asked Malcolm, turning to Jack.

"Yes sir, we are virtually a hundred per cent sure that all the photographs were taken in the tower."

"Did we find any other blood apart from Stephen's?"

"We have found minute traces of blood, but it's not enough to identify, I'm afraid."

"Have we matched any of the photos to missing kids that we know of?"

"Not at the moment," replied Malcolm." But I think you were dealing with missing persons, weren't you Alan?"

"Yes sir, I spent all day there. Only two boys of similar age have gone missing in the last ten years, but they both came from Etwell. One of those is Stephen and the other is..."

"Derek Walsh," said Malcolm, interrupting. "I'm sorry Alan for stealing your thunder."

Malcolm went on to explain how he had met Derek's sister June and the events of the day.

"Don't you think that's a bit of a coincidence guv, two murders in ten years and both boys from the same village?" said one officer.

"We don't know the other boy was murdered," said another.

"What do you think, a ten-year-old walks off into the sunset and starts a new life stacking shelves at Sainsbury's and nobody notices? Get real."

"OK, OK, let's remember we're all on the same side," said Claire Billings.

"Getting back to Stephen, sir. Can we definitely say that he was killed in the tower?"

"I can answer that," said Jack." The Initial autopsy report stated that the body was covered in small contusions, grazes if you will. As you saw from the photograph Stephen was strapped to the stone cross. Rather like a crucifixion. It was his body scraping on the stone cross that caused the abrasions. However that was not the cause of death. The large amount of blood found at the base of the stone cross and the autopsy report are consistent with severe anal haemorrhaging."

"Are you saying this boy was buggered to death?"

"Well, I wouldn't put it quite like that."

"How the bloody hell would you put it?"

"Hold on a moment!" shouted Claire.

"I'm sorry, I shouldn't have said that," said the officer.

"There's one thing more you should know," said Jack. "Stephen had traces of Temazepam in his body. Temazepam is a drug that some of you may have experienced before. It is very often injected as a pre-med before you have an operation. This would have made Stephen more manageable but still conscious. There were no needle marks on the body, so we can only presume the drug was taken orally, either by force or deception."

Sounds of disgust echoed round the room.

"What do you mean exactly?" asked Malcolm.

"It could have been injected into a sweet or an apple

or anything like that and the person would be none the wiser."

"That's very interesting," said Alan. The room fell quiet and all eyes turned towards him.

"Are we talking about the same thing, Alan?" asked Mr Wilkes.

"Oh no. I mean yes sir. It's that drug Mr Digweed mentioned, Tez… amepaz or whatever it was. It's been used before."

"How do you know that, Sherlock?" said Norman, trying to lighten the proceedings.

"Well sir, I know you said only find out about boys missing in the London area, but apart from Derek Walsh and Stephen Jennings there were two others who went missing about the same time as Derek, perhaps a year or so earlier, and they came from the same village. It used to have a coal mine and cotton mill. It's called…" He fumbled through his notebook desperately searching for the details.

"Are here it is, Boothstown, near Manchester. One boy was found naked at the side of the road. He had been badly abused and that drug was found in his system." Alan was still trying to piece together all the notes he had made.

"What about the other boy?" said Malcolm.

"He was never found. He went missing about a month after the first boy was found. I've got it all written down here somewhere.

I went to general registry and picked up all the files they had on the two cases, and I've asked Manchester police to send us their files on both boys. I also drew the file on Derek Walsh."

"On whose authority did you do that?" said Mr Wilkes, tongue in cheek. If he was hoping to embarrass Alan, he would have a long wait.

"Oh I just gave your name sir. I hope that was all right," replied Alan.

"Perfectly all right Alan. Well done. Now how about some ideas on how we are going to identify these boys from the photographs?"

"Well guv, I know we're seeing your mate, the one whose wife was a local teacher. Perhaps we can compare the photographs and see if they match."

"What about showing them to the schools?"

"Don't be bloody stupid, you can't show photographs like that to teachers. It would be all over the press in five minutes," said another.

"What about if we invited the head of each school to a private showing of the photographs?" said Claire Billings.

"Now that sounds more like it," replied Malcolm. "How many schools are there around here, anyway?"

"Haven't a clue," replied Claire, "but I'll find out."

"It's got to be quicker than visiting each school in

turn. It would take forever. This way we could cover two hundred schools at a time."

"There's no guarantee that the boys are local anyway."

"You're right, but let's presume they are. In the meantime, Jack, can you tell me how old these boys in the photographs are?"

"Actually I've had a bit of luck there. A friend of mine is an expert on age analysis and he is convinced that they're all under ten years of age."

"Stephen wasn't. He was nearly thirteen," said Norman.

"But he was small for his age," replied Claire.

"Well at least that narrows it down to just primary schools."

The room was beginning to buzz.

"OK settle down," said Malcolm. "First things first. Claire, can you find out exactly how many primary schools we are dealing with here? We'll start with the local schools first. Get onto the local education authority and get that started, will you?"

"How are we going to get teachers there in the first place? We can't use a police building. Half of them wouldn't turn up on principle, a bunch of left-wing trendies most of them."

"OK, find a suitable venue. A hall. Out of town somewhere. We can arrange transport, that's no problem."

"There is just one problem, sir" said an officer. "What are we going to tell them the meeting's about?"

"Good point. If we tell them the truth before the meeting it'll be all over the press. We'll sort that later Claire, OK?"

"OK guv," replied Claire. "Anything else?"

"Yes, chase up those files from Manchester and make sure the office door lock is changed. I also want reflective screens on the windows, you know the stuff they put on to stop people looking in. Remember everyone" – Malcolm raised his voice above the chatter – "not one word outside this office. Is that clear?"

Malcolm turned to leave. "One other thing, for your eyes and ears only. I'm staying with my old mate the Reverend Daniel Carter. Claire's got the number. It is not to be given to anyone else."

"Is that so you can be closer to God, guv?" said an officer.

"He can't get any closer than he is right now," said Wilkes, who was standing next to Malcolm. "And don't you forget it." He smiled. "Next meeting 8 am sharp. See you tomorrow."

It was late when Malcolm and Norman parked outside Andrew Summers' house. Norman had phoned ahead before they left the office so Andrew was expecting them. He showed his guests through to the lounge, which was already beginning to look as though it needed dusting.

Andrew had already made a pot of coffee and laid it on the table in front of them together with a decanter of brandy and three glasses.

"Mr Summers, erm, Andrew. You've been told why we're here. We need your help. I'm going to show you some photographs. I'll warn you now, they are repulsive. I want to know if you recognise any of the boys in them. It goes without saying that what you're going to see must remain secret. You're a professional. You know what I mean."

"If It's anything to do with that poor boy my grandsons and I found, let me tell you Malcolm, the bastard that did that not only ruined the life of that young boy and his family but he affected my family as well and indeed the whole village, so I want you to know that anything I can do to help you, you only have to ask."

Andrew poured brandy into the three glasses. As he did so he watched Malcolm laying out the photographs on the table in front of him. Before he had finished pouring brandy into the last glass, the tears welled up in his eyes.

"That's him. That's Derek." Andrew looked upwards, tears streaming down his cheeks.

"It's OK," Norman said and he placed his hand on Andrew's shoulder.

"How on earth do people do that to children? What

sort of person does that to a child? That could be my grandson."

Malcolm picked up the faded photograph that Andrew had indicated.

"Are you sure? Are you absolutely sure that this is Derek Walsh?"

Andrew looked at the photograph again and nodded. He looked down at the table and picked up two other photographs.

"These are also of Derek." He handed the photographs to Malcolm. "Who's going to tell June?" He wiped a tear from his cheek.

"I suppose that's my job," replied Malcolm," and I'm not looking forward to it, but she will need to positively identify the photographs of her brother."

"Is it absolutely necessary for her to see the photographs?"

"I'm afraid so. It should be a member of the family if possible."

"I have known June since she was born. I would like to be there when you show her the photographs."

"Thanks. I think I'll get Dan to be there as well. He and June seem to be quite close. Norm, will you ring Dan and ask him to meet us at June's house? You'd better explain what it's all about."

Norman left the room to make his call.

"Do you recognise anyone else in the photographs?"

asked Malcolm.

Andrew shook his head. "I have my late wife's photographs of all the children she taught. There are hundreds of them. I hope they are of use."

"Thank you. I'll make sure you get them back."

Norman returned to the lounge. "June's already at Daniel's place guv. I said we'd go there straight away."

"I'll just lock up," said Andrew.

June knew something was wrong the moment Daniel put the phone down, but when Daniel went to the door a few minutes later and showed Malcolm, Norman and Andrew Summers into the kitchen where she was sitting, she was certain. She leapt to her feet, the tears already cascading down her face.

"You've found him, haven't you? You've found Derek."

"No June, it's not that, well not exactly." Andrew placed his arm around her shoulder. "I'm so sorry, but the police have found some photographs." His voice began to falter and the tears once again began to fall. June faced Andrew and wiped his face with her hand.

"It's all right, I'm OK."

To the onlooker it was hard to judge who was comforting who.

"I must warn you June, the photographs are terrible, but I do have to have a positive identification from a member of the family."

Malcolm laid all the photographs on the table one

by one.

June stared at the photographs, then screamed and slammed her hands onto the table. Andrew tried to hold her, but she forced him off.

"What have they done to him? He's just a boy!"

June fell into Andrew s arms, and he scooped her up and carried her through to the lounge and laid her on the sofa. Daniel knelt by her side and held her hand. June slowly began to assimilate the vision she had just seen.

"What did they do to my brother?" said June, crying and shaking her head from side to side. Nobody could answer her. June looked at Malcolm and understood his unease.

"You don't have to worry, Malcolm. I know what you're thinking."

Malcolm looked at her. "Am I that obvious?"

"I promise you, I will not breathe a word of what I know. Finding my brother and the bastards that did that is far more important than a few headlines with my name underneath."

"Thank you. You're right, I was worried. We need absolute secrecy on this."

"On one condition," said June.

Malcolm looked at her tear-stained face, not knowing what to expect but fearing the worst. "Go on," he said.

"If you find Derek, whether he is dead or alive, I

want to be there."

"I promise."

Chapter 16

They had all stayed up long into the night, and it was after midnight when Norman took Andrew home. Malcolm had left Dan and June talking in the lounge and gone up to bed. During the evening the conversation had focused, not surprisingly, on relationships and loved ones. Andrew had told of his grief at his wife's premature death and of the strained relationship with his son-in-law and how much he missed his wife's words of wisdom. He spoke also of his grandchildren and his hopes of seeing them again soon.

June had talked about her relationship with her younger brother. They had even laughed when she recalled the tricks he used to play on her and how she had shouted at him on more than one occasion. Then of course there was the anguish she had felt when he went missing. It started Malcolm thinking about his own failed relationship. He missed Alice so much, and it was at times like this that he needed her most of all, but he had never told her. He was always too busy fighting a battle somewhere or sorting out someone else's problems. They thought it would be so different when he left the army, they would have more time for each other, but if anything they saw even less of each other. He thought about what Daniel had said earlier: "It's never too late to make up, to say you're sorry, to change."

On the excuse of going upstairs and changing for bed, Malcolm had rung home, but there had been no reply. Why should there have been, he asked himself? She was entitled to have a life of her own now. He tried her number again just before he went to sleep, but there was still no reply and the answering machine was still switched on, which usually meant she was still out. Again he left no message.

Norman picked Malcolm up early from the cottage the next morning and they arrived in the office just after 7 am. Claire was already at her desk and had methodically ruled off another day off her calendar.

"You're going to miss this job when you go," said Norman.

"Like a bloody toothache. Kettle's just boiled."

Malcolm went into the small office and phoned Lucy again. He was determined to see her. He'd made up his mind. It was he who was being selfish. He loved her and needed her and wanted to be with her. He had told Norman of his intentions on the way to the office, and it was Norman who closed the office door so that he would not be interrupted. Norman sat on the edge of Claire's desk. "He's phoning his wife," he whispered.

"About bloody time too. They're too nice a couple to throw away what they've got."

Claire looked at Norman and beckoned him to come closer. Norman lowered his head and cocked his ear towards her.

"Good job the guvnor's got a friend who can keep secrets," she murmured. They smiled at each other.

Malcolm dialled the number and it rang. "At least the answering machine's not on," he said. The receiver was picked up at the other end and a man's voice said,

"Yeah, who is it? Hello?"

Malcolm heard his wife call out from upstairs,

"Who is it?"

"I don't know. Hello, anyone there? Nobody's saying anything."

"Oh well, if it's that important they'll ring back."

The man replaced the receiver. Malcolm still held the phone against his ear, listening to the monotone hum, then slowly placed the receiver. He was stunned. It had never crossed his mind that she would find someone else so soon, that she would sleep with anyone else. How stupid he was. How naive. That was it then. It was finally over. He had lost everything that he loved and cared about, he also felt anger because he knew he could have done something about it but he was too proud and stubborn. He returned to the main office.

"Everything all right guv?" Norman smiled.

Malcolm didn't answer. He just poured himself a mug of coffee. Norman looked across at Claire and they both realised from the look on Malcolm's face that all was not well.

"How are we doing Claire?" Malcolm asked.

"Everything is up and running. We've received all the papers on Derek Walsh from SO5 and we've also received the papers on those two boys from Manchester. I've got a copy of the autopsy report, but it doesn't tell us much more than Jack told us last night. All that information, as well as every known local pervert, is being fed into the computers as we speak. I have a locksmith arriving here at nine o'clock and the engineers will fit screens to the windows this afternoon. I'm still waiting for the education department to work out how many primary schools they have. It would seem that they don't actually keep that information, but we're working on it. Oh one other thing sir, there was a message on the answering machine from someone in Manchester. I presume it's about those files they've sent. He said he'll ring back at ten. He said it was important."

By 8 am all the team had assembled for the early morning meeting. Claire brought them up to date with what had happened before handing over to Malcolm.

"Last night Derek Walsh was positively identified as one of the boys in the photographs," she said. Malcolm passed the three photographs of Derek Walsh around the table.

"That still leaves the other boys, guv," said one of the officers.

"That's why it's important to get the teachers all together in one place and try and identify them. We'll start with the local schools and take it from there."

"I'm still working on a venue, guv. Would it matter if it were off the district? I'm thinking of a hall I know in a village in Sussex. It's only just over the border."

"Work on it and come back to us by this afternoon. Now, you're all going to have about half a dozen perverts each to visit. I want them turned over properly. I don't give a shit about them or their civil rights, if they give you any aggro, nick 'em, and don't forget to tell the neighbours why you're there. Oh, one last thing, we borrowed several hundred photographs of local children who went to the village school. It's a long shot, but I need someone to take them up to the lab so they can compare them with the ones we found."

"Leave that to me sir. I'll arrange that."

"Thanks Claire. Now, has anybody got any good news to share with us before we start turning over the pervs?" said Malcolm.

Alan nervously raised his hand.

"Go on Sherlock, what other ideas have you got?" said Norman mockingly.

"You're fined," said Malcolm. "He's had more ideas than you."

Norman laughed and immediately produced another bottle of Jameson's from his briefcase. The laughter rippled round the table.

"Too early for me," said one.

"Yeah give it half an hour," replied another.

"I don't know exactly," said Alan.

"Come on spit it out, don't let this old fart put you off, Just say what you feel," Malcolm said reassuringly.

"Well it's like this sir," Alan began tentatively. "If these paedophiles have been doing this for a long time without being caught, and if Mr Digweed is right it's been going on for several years, well, why did they leave Stephen's body in a place where it was bound to be found eventually?"

The room fell silent and everyone's attention was focused on Alan.

"What are you getting at, son?"

"Well, if they're so clever and the same people are responsible for the deaths of both, why did they suddenly make a mistake?"

"What are you getting at Alan?" said Claire. "We don't have all day."

"Well as I was saying, they've been very clever up until now..."

"Chapter three," said Norman, chuckling to himself,

"Give the lad a chance," said Malcolm.

"I think they were disturbed," Alan blurted out.

Everyone looked at Alan, and Malcolm sat back in his chair.

"Go on son. Just say what you want to say and the rest of you shut up."

"Sir, I don't think they would risk driving round the streets with a dead body in the back, specially with so much blood around. I think they were going to dispose of the body in the graveyard and were disturbed by the people who desecrated the grave of that Jewish chap."

"Hold on Alan. Do you think they are going to calmly walk over half a mile with a body over their shoulders? Remember we found no tyre marks at the scene."

"No, you don't understand sir. They used the Old Alleyway."

"What alleyway?" said Norman. "I don't remember seeing any alleyway near the church."

"It's just across the road from the old tower. It runs alongside the school. It used to be an old drovers' trail. It's where they took the cattle down to the village pond to water them in the old days. It hasn't been used for years and it's overgrown, but it leads right up to the main road, directly opposite the banqueting hall where Stephen's body was found."

Malcolm tried to interrupt, but Alan was on a roll and was now pacing up and down.

"I'm sure these people intended to dispose of Stephen in the graveyard. After all, what better place to hide a body than in a graveyard?" Malcolm once again tried to interrupt, but he cut him off. "I know what you're going to say sir. They still have to cross a busy main road. Well at three o'clock in the morning the traffic is non-existent, and from the alleyway you have four hundred yards of uninterrupted vision which would give anyone plenty of time to get across the road without being seen."

"You know that for a fact, do you Alan?" Malcolm eventually managed to say.

"Yes I do sir. I was there at three o'clock this morning and there was hardly any traffic at all." Alan at last ran out of breath and he stood looking at the team. They in turn were all looking at him.

Norman leant across the table towards his old friend. "You know Boss, he could just be right." he said quietly.

"Let me get this straight Alan. What you're saying is that these perverts intended to bury Stephen right from the start in the graveyard near the tower."

"Yes sir."

"And you're saying they were disturbed by the Nazi yobs desecrating the grave."

"Yes sir."

"And what you're suggesting is, that these perverts have done this before."

"Yes sir."

"And you believe that there may be a boy's body buried somewhere in the graveyard, possibly that of Derek Walsh who disappeared several years ago."

"Yes sir."

"Do you have any idea what you're asking me to do? Don't answer that."

Malcolm thought for a moment and then turned to Claire. "Claire, I want a forensic team to search that alleyway. I want a fingertip search, and I want it started this morning."

Claire started scribbling notes.

"I want another team to check every grave to see if they've been tampered with recently."

"We can't open every grave in the cemetery, boss."

"No you're right. We'll concentrate on the old graveyard. The new one is too open. If a grave has been tampered with It must be near the tower."

"If it's there at all," replied Claire, sounding a note of caution.

"Not necessarily sir," interjected one of the other officers. "Suppose they were going to use the freshly-dug grave of Mrs Schneider. I mean you wouldn't have to dig down too far, the grave's already dug, a couple of feet perhaps, then put Stephen in the pit and cover him up."

"Sadly, that's not beyond the realms of possibility," said Claire.

Malcolm recalled a half-forgotten conversation. "Some of these graves look well cared for. You said so yourself Norman."

"That's right." Norman also remembered the conversation. "Dan said something about a historical society. He also said he had never seen anyone in the graveyard."

"Claire, get someone to check with the library and find out who the local historical expert is. And another thing, when you contact the lab, find out if there's a way of looking into a grave without opening it. Remind me to ask Dan if he has burial records, they might come in handy. Let Alan deal with the lab, after all he started this."

"One thing guv. I don't want to seem rude, but how long has your friend been vicar here?"

"About three years. Why?"

"It seems strange that his predecessor knows nothing of what was going on in his church, and then he goes and gets himself killed in a mysterious fire. You know the insurance company never paid out. I don't mean any offence guv, he's your friend an' all."

"No offence taken. Let's find out all about the

Reverend Winterbourne and get all the papers on the fire."

Malcolm rose from his chair. "OK, get to it. The next meeting will be tonight at six o'clock. Claire, can I have a word?"

Claire followed Malcolm him the office.

"Claire, I want you to handle the enquiry into the Reverend Winterbourne, and while you're at it make a few discreet enquiries about Daniel. If you find out anything, I want to know right away."

"Leave it to me guv. By the way, don't forget you have that bloke ringing you at ten."

"Hello. Is that DI Cammock?" said a mature voice on the phone.

"Yes it is. Who am I speaking to please?"

" My name is Don Yapley. Until about eighteen months ago I was a Detective Chief Superintendent in Manchester CID."

"So how can I help you guvnor?"

"It's a long time since anyone called me that, please call me Don. Listen Inspector, ten years ago I was a DCI working on the disappearance of a ten-year-old boy from one of our local mining communities. His name was Dominic Brewer. He was never found. A month previously an eleven-year-old boy was found dead at the side of the road in the same village. He had been violently sexually abused. His name was Russell Downs."

"I know that, I sent for the files."

"Yes I know you did, Malcolm. I had those files flagged. I still have a few friends left in records and when your team requested them, I was informed."

"I don't understand. Why would you do that? Have you got something to add to what's in the files?"

"I don't want to talk on the phone, Malcolm. I would like to come down and talk to you in person this afternoon. There's a flight that gets me into Gatwick at about 1.30. I'll meet you in the bar at the Gatwick Hilton. I can assure you it's very important."

"This isn't some kind of wind up, is it?"

"I wish it was. I couldn't be more serious if I tried. Will you meet me?"

"Yes OK, but if this turns out to be some kind of practical joke... Let me tell you Don, my sense of humour is running short. I hope that's clear."

"Very clear. One more thing – I don't want this telephone call or our conversation logged anywhere on your system. I will explain everything when I see you."

The phone went dead, leaving Malcolm still wondering whether it was a joke or not. In some way he rather hoped it was. The alternative was beginning to worry him.

Chapter 17

The journey to Gatwick didn't take long, and Norman parked in the car park adjacent to the Hilton Hotel.

"So what you're saying is that this might turn out to be a complete load of bollocks. It's a bit cloak and daggerish if you ask me."

"As I told Mr Yapley on the phone, I'm not fond of surprises and I've had more than enough for one day."

"Why, what else has happened? Or shouldn't I ask."

Norman followed his boss past reception and into the bar. He was beginning to think he wasn't going to get a reply of any kind, but then Malcolm spoke.

"When I phoned Alice this morning some bloke answered the phone."

"Who was it?"

"I'd had thought that was pretty obvious, wouldn't you?"

"No. It could have been anybody."

" Look, I know you mean well mate but who do you know who makes house calls at seven o'clock in the morning?"

Norman realised that this was not the time to pursue this particular conversation and not very subtly changed the subject.

"So how are we going to recognise this ex-guvnor from the counties? Tweed suit, brown brogues and one of those double-breasted army coats, the ones that make you look like Colonel Blimp, complete with riding crop and tweed hat - what d'you reckon?"

"I don't know. He shouldn't be too difficult to recognise, after all we are detectives."

"Well it would appear you've dipped out this time, Inspector."

Both men spun round to face the man they that they had just walked past. He was not at all what either of them had expected. Donald Yapley was tall, frail and completely bald. At a guess this was not through natural hair loss but due more to some form of chemotherapy. Even the light blue track suit he was wearing appeared to be several sizes too big. He held a driving licence in one hand and in the other a baseball cap, which he was busy trying to push into his pocket.

"Don Yapley," he said. "It used to be a warrant card,

but this is the best I can offer you."

"Thanks for coming." Malcolm shook his outstretched hand.

"I know I'm not what you expected, Inspector. I didn't expect to look like this myself so soon after retirement. I'll explain later."

Don held out his hand to Norman who shook it.

"Oh, this is DC Norman Harris. I hope you don't mind him being here."

"Please to meet you, guv."

"Thanks for reminding me of my glory days, but it just Don now. Shall we sit down? Now what can I get you?"

"Coffee will do nicely."

"Will you have something to go with it? A brandy perhaps?"

"Oh, go on then," replied Malcolm. "I'm not driving."

Don took a twenty-pound note from his pocket and handed it to Norman. "Would you do the honours, Norman?"

"Of course, Don." Norman walked over to the bar to order the drinks. He realised that it was just a ruse to get rid of him for a few moments so they could speak in confidence.

"I was intrigued by your telephone call," said Malcolm, breaking the ice.

Don Yapley sat back in his chair studying the man

seated opposite him. He had come too far to back out now. After all, he had nothing to lose.

"I'll come straight to the point, Malcolm. I don't have much time. I'm booked on the 4.10 flight back to Manchester."

Malcolm looked at his watch. It was already 2 pm.

"I'd like Norman to be in on this, if that's OK with you," he replied.

"Not at all. So long as you're sure you know you can trust him."

"Of course. He said this was a bit cloak and daggerish, and I think he's probably right."

"I know it sounds like that, but if when I'm finished you think I'm a crank, then we'll just walk away and pretend it never happened. Is that OK with you?"

"Well you've certainly got my attention."

At that point Norman rejoined them with the drinks. "Is it OK if I join you?" At their nods, he distributed the brandies and sat down.

"Early in 1988 a ten-year-old boy left his school in the village of Boothstown to walk the half mile or so to his home," Don began. "He was never seen again. I was a DCI at the time and I know what you're going to say, CID don't usually deal with missing person enquiries, but Dominic's parents were friends of mine. Headquarters wanted me to offload it, but when your dad is a local councillor and on the police committee you can do what you damn well like. Don't get me wrong, as I said the Brewer family are nice people and I was glad to help."

"What has this got to do with my investigation?"

"Let me finish and then you can draw your own conclusions. A few weeks after Dominic had gone missing we were still none the wiser. He seemed to have vanished off the face of the earth. Little more than a month later, the half-naked body of a boy was found at the side of the road on the outskirts of the village. His name was Russell Downs. He was fourteen years old. Now to start with, the officers at the scene felt that it might have been a bizarre game of chicken and it was dealt with as a road traffic accident, but the autopsy showed that he had been brutally sexually abused. Because of the delay vital clues may have been lost."

"I still don't see a connection with what we're are investigating, apart from that the two boys were local."

"The autopsy on Russell showed that he had been given Temazepam and that at some stage his hands and feet had been bound."

"Oh shit," said Norman.

"Precisely. But that's not all. The entire investigation was taken over by headquarters."

"Is that unusual?"

"I know DCIs are two a penny in the Met, but in the sticks we're gods, and for me not to deal with a murder on my own patch – yes, it was unusual. When I made enquiries a few weeks later the investigation had already been wound down."

Malcolm was about to say something, but Don held up his hand.

"Bearing in mind we don't get anywhere near the number of major incidents that you do. I mean, a murder of a young boy out in the sticks is..."

Don took a swallow from his brandy glass, holding it with both hands. His hands trembled as he raised the glass to his lips and he wiped the dribble of liquid from his chin. "Damn it," he said, under his breath. Malcolm and Norman pretended not to notice, but Don knew they were just saving him embarrassment. He settled back and continued.

"When I eventually got to look at the report on Russell Downs' murder I was convinced it had been weeded, you know statements you would expect to be included weren't."

"Did they give any reason for closing down the investigation early?"

"Only that they had exhausted all their enquiries. One thing I forgot to mention, which is very important. The boys lived less than a mile apart and attended the same school, and their families attended the same church. All In all they were two ordinary boys who came from ordinary loving families, and both of them were happy and popular in school. So why were the two enquiries dealt with separately?"

"You're joking!"

Whatever doubts Malcolm may have had about meeting Donald Yapley were now dispelled.

"I may not have been the greatest detective that ever lived, far from it," Don continued, "but even a carrot-crunching ex-detective like me would guess that when in the space of a few weeks, -- two boys who are not only from the same village, the same school and the same church, one is found murdered and the other disappears, It doesn't take a brain of Britain to consider that they may be linked."

"I would have thought that was obvious," said Malcolm. "I'm sorry. Go on."

"So there I was, a DCI, God to all those beneath me, and I was having my strings pulled, and I didn't like it."

"What did you do about it?"

"Nothing! Oh I made the right noises, but my wife urged me to keep a low profile, don't rock the boat and all that. You see my wife is a social climber. She always wanted me to be Chief Constable."

"So what was the end result?" asked Norman in a matter of fact way.

"The end result was that a possible – no, probable – murder was reduced to a missing person enquiry and handled for the most part by the local beat officer. I have to say that it was without doubt a very thorough investigation. The area was searched by volunteers and house-to-house enquiries were carried out by the uniform officers, but they didn't have the backing or the resources of headquarters."

Donald lifted the coffee pot to pour himself some more coffee, but his hand started to shake again and Norman reached forward and took hold of it.

"Leave it to me guv." He felt the pot and it was cold.

"I'll get some fresh coffee." Norman left the table and took the cups with him.

"Are you all right?" said Malcolm, leaning towards Don.

"Thanks for asking, it's all right. I won't pass out on you just yet. I've got a few more months hopefully. That's if the doctors are right."

"Oh God, I'm so sorry."

"I've got a tumour you see. They can't operate. It's gone too far. I started having chemo, but I felt so bloody dreadful I stopped it. I'd rather die with some dignity."

At that point Norman returned to the table with a fresh pot of coffee and two new glasses of brandy. "Here we go then," he said cheerfully.

Don raised his fresh glass of brandy to Norman in thanks and continued his story.

"You see, what you have to understand is that Boothstown is a very small community and everyone knows each other. A stranger stands out like a sore thumb. You can fire a cannon down the high street after seven o'clock and not hit anybody. Which made it even more strange that nobody saw Dominic Brewer after he left school. I was under a lot of pressure to close the enquiry quickly. Lack of funds was given as the excuse. I kept in touch with the Brewers – as I said, they were friends. It's through them that I got to know Ernest Cheal. He was the vicar of the parish church, but he was getting on in years. He must have been over seventy, and he took it very badly. He used to ring me nearly every week. Oh, I forgot to mention, Dominic was an altar boy."

Don took another sip of his brandy and allowed it to wash over his tongue. He then took a sip of coffee.

"So what you're saying is that someone high up in headquarters staff blocked the investigation of Russell Downs for reasons best known to themselves?"

"It could just be for financial reasons. After all, this government is always cutting the budget."

"I was beginning to believe that myself," replied Don. "Whether I did or whether I didn't. It made me feel better."

Don paused for a moment and looked around him. There was no one seated near them apart from a young couple who looked as though they were backpacking around the world.

"About two months later, I had a phone call from the Brewers to say that the old vicar had died and would I like to pay my respects at his funeral, which I did," Don went on. "At the funeral I was introduced to his replacement, a nice young chap. Well during our conversation he happened to mention that he was surprised that Ernest Cheal's assistant hadn't turned up for the funeral. The Brewers were very surprised. They never knew he had an assistant, and they're big church people. They made some enquiries and it turned out this helper came from a sort of theological college not far from the village. You know, a place where you train for missionary work. He apparently came at weekends and started a swimming club, but apparently it closed as soon as it started."

"How do you know that?" asked Norman.

"Give him a chance," said Malcolm.

"I don't blame you. I'm a bit long-winded these days."

"I'm sorry guv."

"Well, that's just it. Nobody seemed to have any knowledge of this swimming club or the vicar's assistant, so I asked the local bobby to make some enquiries for me. He was a local man and his son attended the same school as the other two boys. After about a week he found a couple of boys that belonged to this swimming club. They only stayed in the pool about half an hour.

It would appear that our trainee vicar couldn't keep his hands off them. The boys were too embarrassed to tell anybody and didn't want to make a statement to police. I decided to make a few enquiries of my own about this trainee. After all, nobody even knew his name and he was never mentioned during the investigation."

Don took another sip of brandy from the trembling glass.

"I contacted this college. It wasn't far away. I spoke to a fella who said he was the secretary. He said he didn't know what I was talking about, but he would look into it and ring me back."

"And did he?" interrupted Norman. "Sorry guv, go on."

"No he didn't, but my Chief Superintendent did. He explained to me in words of one syllable that if I wished to continue in the CID, or the police force for that matter, I should direct my enquiries to crime issues and not missing persons. When I fronted him about having had a phone call from this college, he denied all knowledge of it."

"You didn't believe him then?" said Norman.

"Did I bollocks."

"What did you do about it?" asked Malcolm.

"I rang the college several times after that, just to see what reaction I would get. They always said they would phone me back, but they never did. Until one day I received a call from the college apologising for not contacting me sooner. They said they had no idea who the man was, but as their students were now doing missionary work that was the end of the matter. I still wasn't convinced. So I decided to use a different tack. I made out I was a student doing a thesis on missionary work and could they help me."

"So far Don, what you've told us is strange, it may even be corrupt, but you'd have a hard job proving it and the only connection with my enquiry is that the drug Temazepam was used in both cases."

"You're quite right Malcolm, but bear with me. The college sent me a load of bumph about their history and what their aims were."

Don removed a pamphlet from inside his track suit and laid it on the table. He opened it. It was dated 1967, and on the inside cover was a photograph of two young men dressed in monks' habits. He pushed the pamphlet towards Malcolm.

"I don't get it, Don. What am I supposed to be looking at?"

Don pointed to the photograph.

"The one on the left is Maurice Flower, known to his friends and enemies as Petal."

"I still don't get it what you're driving at."

"Fifteen years ago, Maurice Flower was my Chief

Superintendent."

Malcolm and Norman just sat there, not knowing what to say. Now they understood only too well why Don Yapley was being so secretive. But worse was to follow.

"I went to see him and told him what I had found out. He denied everything of course, but a few weeks later I was transferred to Headquarters duty and promoted to Superintendent. I remained there until I retired on ill health. I was promoted to Chief two months before I left. It was a present for keeping quiet for all those years and not rocking the boat. Nothing was ever said, there were no admissions, but I knew. You know, when I joined this job, the then Chief Constable talked about integrity. Well I sold mine for a fat pension and to keep a pretentious wife happy."

Don sat back, lowered his head and took a deep breath. He clearly felt that a great load had been removed from his shoulders.

"I don't know what to say to you," said Malcolm. " I still don't see how this relates to our crime."

"I don't know exactly what your crime is Malcolm, but I can guess. You didn't request the papers on these two boys just because you had nothing to read."

"But what is the connection with our job?" asked Norman.

"The name of the other man in the photograph is

Winterbourne. Until his death a few years ago he was the vicar of St Andrew's, where your boy was murdered. I think you might know his brother, the former Home Secretary."

Malcolm and Norman looked at each other. "What is going on here guv?" said Norman in disbelief.

"There's one more thing more you should know. Maurice Flowers was made Chief Constable when Winterbourne was Home Secretary. He has since retired. These people, whoever they are, have some very powerful friends. So be careful and watch your back."

The three men sat in silence as Norman refilled their coffee cups.

"I'm going to have to go. I've got to check in. This is my home number. Ring me any time, but don't tell my wife what it's about." He placed his card on the table and held out his hand.

"Does your wife know you're here?" said Malcolm, as he shook his hand.

Don laughed. "She thinks I'm playing dominoes down the legion. Not that she cares where I am really, so long as I don't embarrass her."

Don shook hands with Norman. "Look after your boss and watch his back." Norman nodded and gripped his hand a little tighter.

"And you're wrong. I don't possess a tweed hat." Don laughed, pulled on his baseball cap and walked off towards the departure terminal. "Don't forget, Malcolm. Time is ticking by. I'd like a result!" he called.

"What did he mean by that?" asked Norman.

"I'll tell you later. Right now we need to get back to the office."

Chapter 18

On the journey back from Gatwick, Malcolm phoned Chief Superintendent Wilkes and arranged to meet him at the office. He also phoned Claire Billings and told her to make sure that the small office was empty. It was to be a private meeting, just the four of them.

When they arrived at the office the door was locked, but before Norman could knock, the door was opened by Alan. Inside, they could see that Wilkes had already arrived.

"That's the first time I've ever had to ask to enter my own murder squad office, Malcolm. Is it absolutely necessary?" said Wilkes, with just a touch of annoyance in his voice.

"I'm sorry about that guv. I'll make sure you're given

a key before you go," said Claire diplomatically. "I've asked Alan to act as doorman and answer the phones while we have this meeting in your office. The coffee is already in there."

Wilkes was already heading for the office, followed by Norman.

"Why is he in such a bad mood?" Malcolm whispered to Alan.

"Not only could he not get in here, he was refused entry to the station yard by a PC with less service than me, if that's possible. The PC asked for identification and Mr Wilkes had left his warrant card at home. He nearly got nicked."

"Are you going to be long, Inspector?" Wilkes called from the office.

"Remember Alan, we do not want to be disturbed and whatever you overhear must never be repeated. Is that clear?"

"Yes sir, I understand, I think."

"By the way, have Forensics come back with anything from your alley?"

"Not yet sir. They said they would ring when they'd completed the search."

Malcolm nodded his appreciation, entered the small office and shut the door behind him. He and Norman went over the details of their meeting with Don Yapley and the incredible and disturbing story he had told them.

"I can hardly believe it. I mean thriller writers couldn't script something like this," said a stunned Mr Wilkes. "But we've been here before, haven't we Claire?"

"What do you mean?" enquired Norman.

"In the mid-eighties Claire and I were working Vice out of Vine Street. I was a DS then. We were trying to clean up the meat rack in Piccadilly. You know, where all the rent boys hang out. We heard on the grapevine that some of the boys were being used by a high-class pimp."

"Nothing new in that guvnor, been going on for years."

"But not quite on this scale," said Claire.

"Anyway, we managed to get into a couple of the rent boys and what they told us was quite unbelievable. They were being rented out to VIPs, and it has to be said were earning very good money."

"That's OK if you don't mind flogging your arse and are prepared to run the risk of dying from aids," said Norman bitterly.

"Some of these boys had been homeless on the street or in care homes for months, sometimes years," snapped Claire at Norman. "Nearly all of them had left home or been thrown out after years of abuse from their parents. Is it any wonder they get dragged into prostitution or drugs? And besides, what else has this supposedly classless, caring society done for them?"

"You're right," he said. "Some of these kids have never stood a chance."

"Anyway, I'll come off my soap box. These boys gave us names, dates, places. They drew diagrams of the houses they had been taken to, even the index numbers of the cars that transported them. You would not believe the names we were given."

"Well, don't keep us in suspense. Who were these pervs?" asked Norman impatiently.

"It involved MPs, government ministers, members of the clergy, the armed forces, judges, high-powered business people and even a couple of senior police officers. It was like a Who's Who of paedophiles. What was the name of the operation, Claire?"

"Operation Orchid."

"That's it. We were really doing well, gathered loads of information and we were really discreet and about to start nicking them when they closed us down."

"You weren't discreet enough," interrupted Claire.

"We had those bastards bang to rights and they shut us down."

"Who closed you down?" asked Norman.

"We had been up and running for some time, then one afternoon this commander from special branch turns up with a couple of guys supposedly from the DPP and we were told that the investigation would cease at once and all papers were to be given to the DPP for filing. Well you can imagine how the team felt about it. It was obvious that our investigation was rattling a few cages in high places, so they closed us down. Just like that."

"They must have told you why, given you some sort of reason?" said Norman.

"Oh they gave us a reason all right," said Claire sarcastically. "It was not in the public interest."

"That's bloody outrageous!" said Norman angrily.

"I'm not surprised," said Malcolm. "It's never happened to me, but a colleague of mine in South London had an investigation shut down."

"Was that a paedophile investigation as well?" asked Norman.

"Yes, very similar. It was all right when the only people being arrested were teachers and social workers, but when the enquiries shifted to the Houses of Parliament It was stopped immediately. You must remember these people will stop at nothing to protect their own reputations, and they have the money and position to do something about it."

"What reason did they give, not in the bleeding public interest? Not in their bloody interest more like," said Norman, "Isn't that what they said about the North Wales child abuse enquiry in '97?"

"And we're suggesting that at the very least that a former Home Secretary, who is still an MP, and a former chief constable may at the very least either be involved in murder or have covered up information relating to the murder and or disappearance of two boys up north and god knows what down here. Jesus, it's a real can of worms."

"I want you to know something right from the start," said Wilkes. "There will be no cover up on this investigation. I don't give a shit if the commissioner himself is involved, I'll nick him personally."

"I think you'd be in the queue for that honour, guv," said Claire bitterly.

"Have you still got that list of paedophiles from the eighties, Clare?"

"Yes guv, I took photocopies of the statements at the time, but none of our names show up."

"Do you keep your own private lists now?" asked Norman.

"Do you remember an operation called Hedge?" asked Wilkes. Both men shook their heads. "It was a bit before your time, but in the early eighties there had been several high-profile child abductions and murders and the politicians decided that the police should do something about it, so they did. They used crime squads, TSG and anyone they could get to target known or suspected paedophiles. Well, the information they gathered was staggering, and it was about to be actioned when it was shut down just as quickly as it started. That info from Operation Hedge was available right up until the end of the eighties or early nineties, but it has become virtually impossible to access now, hence people of your generation have never heard of it. That's why I and Claire took copies."

"That's very naughty, you could get told off for that," said Norman.

"I remember one strange story. A young TSG officer had been following this known paedophile around for some time, and another guy they couldn't identify. That was until he went to his local church for a wedding rehearsal and there standing in front of him was the mysterious man also known as the vicar."

"Was he one of those on the list to be actioned?"

"I can't remember. I do remember several years later a fifteen-year-old boy went missing and it was strongly believed that the vicar and the gravedigger were responsible and that the boy is buried in the churchyard, but there was no police action."

"I wonder why," said Malcolm

"Not in the fucking public interest, is it?" snorted Norman.

"What are we going to tell the troops?"

"Nothing at this stage, but we must emphasise the need for strict secrecy. We'll tell them when they need to know."

"Yes I agree," said Malcolm. "I see the new locks

have been fitted and the window screens are in place. Well that's a start. By the way, any reference to Donald Yapley and his involvement with this enquiry, even his telephone calls, I want removed."

"Consider it done."

"Just one problem, sir. How are we going to make enquiries on Winterbourne and Flower without causing suspicion? I mean you can't ring up special branch or MI5 and ask them what dirt they've got on a previous Home Secretary and his mate the former Chief Constable of Greater Manchester without causing just a little surprise."

"Good point. For the moment we'll let sleeping dogs lie until we're a bit further forward with our enquiries. I've got a press briefing in an hour, so let's get on with the office meeting. You never know, someone might have some good news for a change."

They went into the main office, where Alan was busy on the phone. He looked up, smiled and clenched his fist in a triumphant salute. Then he put down the phone and leapt to his feet.

"That was the search team, sir. They've found traces of blood and two sets of footprints that they believe match those found in the tower."

"What's he going on about, Norman?" said Wilkes.

"Well, Sherlock reckons they may have carried Stephen from the tower along the alley and over the main road to dispose of him."

"And he was right," said Malcolm. "Well done Alan. Have the rest of the team arrived?"

"Yes sir, they're in the canteen."

"Would you like to get them, so we can all share your information?"

"Did you hear any of our conversation, Alan?"

"Yes sir I did, it was hard not to. Don't worry, I won't talk about it, nobody would believe me anyway." He turned and went off to gather the team from the canteen.

"Were we ever like that?" said Norman with a smile on his face.

"What you mean young, good-looking and keen? I've known you all your service and that is not a description I would apply to you," said Wilkes.

"You know how to hurt a guy."

The team filed back into the office carrying drinks and plates of half-eaten sandwiches. When they were all seated, Wilkes rose from his seat.

"Before we start this meeting, I just want to remind all of you of the need for absolute secrecy. It's very difficult not to discuss the job with your wife or partner. Especially when you've been married for twenty-seven years, as I have."

"Jesus! You only get twelve years for murder," remarked Norman, much to the delight of everyone, including Mr Wilkes.

"You're fined, Norman," said Malcolm, without even looking at him.

"Why am I the only one?" replied Norman.

The laughter died away and the team settled down once more.

"It's not that your partners are untrustworthy, but you offload your burden onto them and they promptly offload it on to someone else. Do not discuss this operation with anybody. I don't want to sound melodramatic, but nobody comes through that door unless he is a member of this team. The door will be kept locked at all times. I don't want anyone just walking in here. Is that quite clear? Right, I'm going downstairs to talk to the press. I'll leave you to get on with it, Malcolm. Give me a ring later on."

"Don't forget your key," said Claire.

"Or your warrant card," said a voice from the table. The ripple of laughter turned into a roar.

"Whoever that was, fine him," laughed Wilkes and left the office.

"OK settle down. We've got a lot to talk about," said Malcolm.

The team quietened. Notebooks were opened in readiness to record any information that they might find useful when talking to informants, witnesses or even suspects.

"Before Alan busts a gut, I think he's got something

to tell us," said Malcolm.

Alan felt his cheeks redden. He tried to hide it, but it was no use. His pale cheeks were now crimson.

"Whatever you do don't ever play poker, Alan," said Malcolm, adding to Alan's embarrassment.

"Except with me," called Norman.

Alan waited for the laughter to subside and then spoke.

"Forensics have found traces of fresh human blood in the alleyway leading from the tower, right across the road towards the burial site. Unfortunately there's not enough to DNA, but they have also found two sets of footprints in the alley that look as though they match those found in the tower. They also found another partial footprint. They can't confirm it at this stage, but they're doing further tests. That's about it for the moment." He sat quietly looking around at his colleagues.

"Well done Alan," said one of the officers.

"Yeah, bloody good job son. Wish I'd thought of it," said another.

"So if Alan's theory is right, it's quite possible that we might have at least one other body buried in the graveyard that shouldn't be there," said Malcolm.

"You mean Derek Walsh, guv," said Claire.

"It could be a whole lot more. We haven't traced the boys in the photographs yet," said another officer.

The mood of the team changed. It seemed to have

dawned on them that if the photographs were anything to go by, they could be dealing with several murdered boys.

"What did forensics come up with, Claire?" said Wilkes. "Have they got any bright ideas on how to find a body in a graveyard? One that shouldn't be there, that is."

"It's a little more difficult than finding a body in a field or under a house. To start with we've already got bodies. Bloody hundreds of them."

"Don't tell me they've drawn a blank."

"Not exactly guv. They gave me the name of a chap at Oxford University, Professor Kennard, and he and his assistant will be here tomorrow morning. I spoke to him on the phone this morning and he got really excited. Basically it's a good excuse for him to test his new equipment."

"That's great Claire. Do you know how his machine works? It's not going to damage anything is it? I don't want to have to replace several hundred gravestones," said Malcolm, his spirits lifted by the good news.

"I haven't the remotest idea guv. He did try to explain how it worked, but he lost me after he said it runs off a car battery." The laughter drifted round the table.

"Well actually," said Alan, realising at once that he should have kept his mouth shut.

"Go on my son, show the sergeant up for the

ignoramus she is."

The team laughed even more, and Alan was goaded into finishing his speech.

"All right, all right. Well it's like a lawnmower with a box of tricks on top. From that, cables are fixed to a computer. It sends out radar waves similar to that of a microwave oven into the ground, only this one won't cook your sausages. It registers anything below ground to a depth of about ten or twelve feet, sometimes more depending on the terrain, and the computer does the rest." He paused for a moment. "I thought everyone knew that." He smiled. "One other thing guv, the Professor wants the area marked out with tape, in five metre sections, so we'll need an early start."

"Do you want to tell them the bad news now guv?" said Norman. The room fell silent for just a moment.

"What, have they cut the overtime already?" said one.

"No, for once we don't have that problem, but that doesn't mean you can rip the arse out of it either."

The team nodded and grunted acknowledgement.

"The fact is, we need to maintain absolute secrecy on this job," said Malcolm. "I want someone to stay here each night until this job is over. I don't want a big thing made of it. I don't want to arouse anyone's suspicions."

"But this is a bloody police station, for Christ's sake. Surely nobody's going to break in here?" said one of the officers. Malcolm, Norman and Claire just stared at the man as he realised at once that his boss was deadly serious.

"The other problem is that I can't pay you any overtime for this. I wish I could tell you otherwise, but I can't. I can't force you to do it. It's got to be on a voluntary basis with no pay."

"I'll do it on one condition," said the same officer. "I don't have to sleep with Norman."

"Thanks very much all of you, I'll make it up to you. Just remember, nobody outside this team comes through that door. I don't give a damn who it is."

"I'll take the first watch sir," said Alan.

"Only after you've bought the first round," said Norman, to great cheers from the rest of the team.

"That's another thing. I don't want any loose talk down the boozer. I'm quite happy if you fancy a drink here in the office, but only after the work is done," said Malcolm.

Everyone was now aware of the seriousness of the situation. They might not have known the reasons why, but they knew it was important.

"Before everyone disappears, have we got any more news?"

"The enquiries regarding the local perverts have drawn a blank so far," replied Claire. "We've still a few more to go, but it should be cleared by tomorrow and negative on the house to house."

"What about a venue for our teachers?" enquired Malcolm.

"I've managed to find one, but it isn't local." Claire was choosing her words very carefully. "I contacted an old friend of mine. He's ex Old Bill and he runs a pub in Sussex, a place called Warninglid. He's got a large hall at the back of his place which will be ideal. It will mean bussing the teachers from the town hall, but it's only half an hour down the motorway."

"That's sounds just what we want. How many teachers are we talking about?"

Claire rummaged through some papers in front of her and produced a sheet of paper with the information she required.

"There are twenty-seven schools in all, including private and special needs, that have boys of the same ages as the ones we're trying to identify."

"That's tremendous, Claire. When can we have the hall?"

"Any time we like. I've also arranged a meeting between Mr Wilkes and the Chairman of Education for tomorrow morning."

"You seem to have taken care of everything. Right you lot, six am start tomorrow. Alan, mind the shop, any problems ring me on my mobile. See you all tomorrow. Thanks for all your hard work."

Malcolm and Norman left the office and returned to

the cottage. They were not surprised to see June still there. She looked very relaxed in Dan's company.

"You've had a long day," said Daniel, already pouring brandy into two glasses.

"Not for me, Dan," said Norman. "I'm going straight home to surprise the wife with the lodger." They all laughed, but Norman saw the fleeting look of pain on Malcolm's face and remembered his friend's problems.

"Thanks for the lift Norman, we might as well meet here tomorrow as we'll be working across the road," said Malcolm.

Norman waved goodbye and left the cottage. Malcolm saw the reaction on June's face to what he had just said and knew he had to tell her. He sat down in the armchair opposite them and allowed the brandy to wash around his mouth.

"I'll need help from both of you tomorrow. There's no easy way of putting this June, but I believe Derek is buried somewhere in the graveyard, possibly near the tower." June squeezed Dan's hand.

"How can I help?" June said.

"By staying well away from the graveyard. If you're seen there people will put two and two together, and I want to keep the lid on this for as long as possible. Dan, I need your permission to search the graveyard. It doesn't entail digging of any kind."

"You've got it. If there's anything else I can do, you

only have to ask."

"There is one more thing. There will be a lot of officers working here tomorrow. Do you mind if we use the cottage as a base?"

"Not at all. I'll prepare some food for them, If that's all right. At least I'll be doing something to help. You will tell me straight away if you find anything?"

"I promise. Now if you'll forgive me, I'm going to have an early night."

They wished each other goodnight and Malcolm left the room. He lay on his bed and in his mind retraced the events of the day, but his thoughts always returned to his wife, and he kept imagining her lying in the arms of another man. He wanted to phone her. He wanted to tell her he was sorry. He wanted to know the truth… No, that was a lie. He didn't want to know the truth. He was frightened to face the truth, because he was afraid of what he might hear, that his marriage was really over.

He drifted off into a restless sleep.

Chapter 19

The next morning Malcolm awoke from a fitful night's sleep, dressed quickly and went outside. He found Norman sitting in his car waiting for him.

"Couldn't you sleep either?" Norman called through the open car window.

"I didn't want to disturb them. June's been up most of the night, I could hear her moving around in the kitchen. Leave your car here and we'll stroll down and join the troops. I know they're here, I could hear them crashing about in the graveyard."

Norman locked his car and together they walked off along the lane towards the old church tower, which was surrounded by police 'DO NOT CROSS' tape.

"Have you told June what we're doing this morning?"

Norman asked inquisitively.

"I can't see as I had much choice, she's only two hundred yards away and I'd prefer to know exactly where she is," Malcolm replied.

"I hope this isn't going to be a waste of time, we're staking a great deal on finding Derek's body here. I just hope for June's sake we get a result." Norman sounded almost apologetic.

They made their way to the end of the lane, where most of the team had arrived and were already busy marking out sections of the cemetery using the blue and white tape they used to cordon off areas. Claire was busy marking out each five-metre section with a steel tape measure. They fixed the tape to small pegs, which were hammered in at the required distances.

"You seem to have everything under control Claire. Is there anything we can do?" asked Malcolm.

"You could rustle up some tea and coffee guv, but apart from that everything's done. I've got the uniform to close off the lane at both ends and I took the liberty of phoning Professor Kennard. Just as well I did because he said he wants to start at eight o'clock sharp."

"It seems I got up early for nothing. I've arranged some refreshments for the lads back at the cottage in the meantime. I'll do what detective inspectors do best, go and make the tea and coffee."

"Thanks guv," the team chorused.

"Will you do me a favour Norman? I know you don't agree with June being involved as much as she is, but she has offered to cook up a bite to eat for everyone. Would you mind getting the makings?"

"Listen guv, about earlier. You know I'll support you in anything you decide to do and that's all I'm saying on the matter, and a bloody good fry up is just what I could do with."

"Thanks mate. Norman's going to organise breakfast. I'll be back at the cottage. Let me know when Professor Kennard arrives."

Malcolm called across the graveyard to Claire. She waved a hand in response and Malcolm strolled back to the cottage.

Later, Malcolm and Norman were sitting in the kitchen with June and Dan, finishing their breakfast.

"That was lovely," said Norman, running a piece of bread round the plate to scoop up the last remnants of his meal.

"I'm glad you enjoyed it. There's more toast if you like."

As she finished speaking, the mobile phone that had lain dormant on the table burst into life. Malcolm answered it.

"Right, thanks a lot" he said and switched it off. "The Professor has arrived and he's already unloading his gear. We're wanted straight away. Thanks for the breakfast. I'll let you know what happens." He was out of the room in a shot.

Norman rose from his chair more slowly, finishing his coffee as he did so. He tried hard not to look at June, but when he did, he saw a frightened girl who seemed not much older than his own daughter trying hard to contain her anxiety. Norman couldn't help himself. He walked over and held her in his arms.

"I'm all right," she said unconvincingly.

"Listen, whatever happens we'll come back and tell you right away. That's a promise, and old farts like me don't break promises."

June was unable to reply. If she had , she knew she would have broken down. Norman left the cottage and joined Malcolm, who was already halfway down the lane.

"Nice girl that," he said with a grin.

Malcolm just smiled at his old friend. It had crossed his mind more than once that his true friends could be counted on the fingers of one hand.

Malcolm's idea of an Oxford professor was similar to that of most other people; a David Bellamy-type character but with a gangling physique, thick glasses, buck teeth and a dress sense that no self-respecting tramp would be seen dead in, plus hair that stood straight up, as though he was one of those cartoon characters who had just been electrocuted.

He would have been a long way from the mark. To start with, Professor Matthew Kennard was only twenty-seven years old. He drove a top of the range Audi estate and wore designer clothes. When Malcolm arrived, he was busy pulling on overalls to cover his suit.

"I'm pleased to meet you professor," said Malcolm. "I'm sorry I wasn't here to meet you personally."

"Nah, don't worry about that Inspector, and call me Matt, everyone else does." The Professor's London accent was even sharper than Norman's.

"Whereabouts in south London are you from, Matt?"

"Born in Balham, gateway to the south, as my old man used to say, bless his cotton socks."

"Call me Malcolm. Now is there anything we can do to help?"

"I could use two of your strong men to lug this bloody machine around for me. It weighs a ton."

"No problem there, we have several volunteers lined up, haven't we lads? I've laid on refreshments for you and your crew whenever you want them."

"We won't need a lot of feeding. It's only me and Rachel and she's into sparrows' food. See what I mean?" Matthew nodded in the direction of Rachel, who was busy attaching wires to a laptop computer and fiddling with dials. She was stunning, and her figure had not gone unnoticed by the team. She would have put most models to shame.

"I know what you're thinking Malcolm, but she's got brains as well as a great arse," said Matthew, with a grin at Rachel. She overheard the remark and just smiled and continued her work.

"I need to calibrate this machine against a fresh grave. You know, one that you know how many people are buried in," said Matthew.

"I know I can help with that. There's a grave in the new part of the cemetery. It's only a few days old and we know that only two people are buried there."

Malcolm took Professor Kennard to the site of Mrs Schneider's grave. "I'll let you get on," he said. "If there's anything else you need, just say."

Professor Kennard and his beautiful assistant were oblivious to his words. They both had headsets on, and the professor was moving a hand-held machine over the grave. They were talking to each other in what Malcolm could only assume was computer speak.

It was nearly midday before the professor and his team had completed the sweep of the old graveyard. They and Norman returned to the cottage, and Malcolm sat at the kitchen table as Norman gave him the news.

"Nothing. Not a sign of anything unusual. There are plenty of dead bodies, but not the one we're looking for. All the bodies in that graveyard have been there for yonks. They're breaking for lunch now. The professor wants to scan the area one more time, just to confirm his findings, but he doesn't hold out much hope."

At that point Professor Kennard and Rachel came into the kitchen.

"You are sure you've got a body buried out there – I mean one that's unaccounted for?" said the professor and sat down at the table. "I'm flippin' knackered. I could do with a beer."

"I'm afraid I'm right out of beer. Will lager do?" said Dan. He stood in the doorway, his white clerical collar clearly visible under his sweater.

"I'm terribly sorry vicar, me and my big mouth. I meant no offence."

"That's quite all right. It's been happening to me quite a lot lately, hasn't it Norman?"

"Don't pick on me Dan. I'm a reformed character."

"I think there's something else you should know, Matt."

Malcolm's tone of voice silenced the brief banter around the table, but June interrupted him.

"The body you're looking for is my brother, professor. You will do your best won't you?"

Professor Kennard hung his head. "I am so sorry. I had no idea."

"In answer to your first question, Matt," said Malcolm, "Nothing is certain. I just believe that somewhere in that graveyard is the body of Derek Walsh, June's younger brother."

"Well we'd better not waste any more time. Let's get on with it."

The Professor stood up and walked out, still drinking his can of lager, and was quickly followed by Rachel, Malcolm and Norman. Dan decided to join them, but before he left he placed his hands on June's shoulder. "I'll come back as soon as there's any news," he said.

It was after six when they completed the final sweep of the graveyard. The Professor began loading his car with his equipment and everyone was looking tired and dejected.

"I'm sorry Malcolm, my first readings were correct," said Matthew. "All the bodies buried in that part of the cemetery can be accounted for. They are spaced apart, as you would expect them to be, even those that have been in the ground for hundreds of years. Even taking into consideration decomposition, the gaps between each body are as you would expect. I suppose what I'm trying to say is that no one has been buried in that cemetery that should not be there. I'm sorry."

"Thanks for all you've done. Look I know it's not what we agreed, but would you be prepared to come back tomorrow and cover the new graveyard?"

"Do you think it's likely he's buried there?"

"Frankly, I just don't know. I was convinced he was here, but obviously I was wrong."

"If your lads can mark out the pitch, we'll give it our best shot. Same time tomorrow then." He closed the tailgate of his car and climbed into the driving seat, Rachel beside him.

"Send everybody home, Norman," said Malcolm. "Get a good night's sleep and a six o'clock start to mark out the new graveyard. Thank them all for me. I'll be at the cottage if there's any problem. By the way, who's watching the office tonight?" He looked and sounded depressed.

"Claire's got that honour," replied Norman.

Malcolm and Dan made their way slowly back to the cottage.

"I don't know Dan, what am I doing wrong? I was convinced Derek was buried out there. It makes sense. Who would think of searching a graveyard for a murder victim?"

"You did."

"Yes, but I still haven't found him, have I?"

"Have faith, old friend. Tomorrow is another day."

The next day Malcolm arrived at the church early and was surprised to find the professor and Rachel already hard at work.

"When did they arrive?" Malcolm asked Norman, who was busy marking out plots with the blue and white tape.

"They arrived at sparrow's fart. They've nearly done half of it already. The professor reckons it's a lot easier over this ground. Don't ask me why, I haven't a clue." He paused for a moment when he saw the disappointment on his friend's face. "They haven't found anything. To be honest, I don't think they will. This part of the cemetery is too open, too overlooked. Anybody burying a body late at night would be seen or heard."

"Nobody heard or saw what happened here the other night, did they?"

Malcolm stood and watched as the professor and his assistant ran the machine over the ground and over the graves in their fruitless search. Before Norman could reply, and just to add to their problems, it started to rain.

"That's all we bloody want!" cried Malcolm in sheer frustration.

The professor came across to where Malcolm was standing. "Don't worry Malcolm, the rain won't affect our readings. I'll be finished in a couple of hours. To be honest, it's not looking too promising."

"I'm sorry I've wasted your time. I know you must be busy. If you send your bill to me, I'll make sure it gets paid."

"Don't be daft Malcolm, a weekend alone with the best-looking scientist in Oxford? I should be paying you." He went off to continue his search.

"I'm going back to the office," Malcolm called across the graveyard to Norman. "See you back there later."

It was late afternoon when all the team assembled back at the office. Some officers were drying their hair, others were wiping the mud from their shoes. Chief Superintendent Wilkes was present and was busy talking on the phone. When he had finished, he replaced the receiver and looked directly at Malcolm.

"We need to talk."

Malcolm followed him into the private office and closed the door.

"That was the Assistant Commissioner, no less. He would like to pop in and see how our investigation is going. A sort of morale boosting visit."

"Well that's jolly nice of him," Malcolm said sarcastically.

"Oh, that's not the best bit. He would like to bring along a friend of his who sits on the Police Consultative Committee. You've heard of him. It's Henry Winterbourne."

"You are bloody joking! They haven't wasted much time. They're worried that we've found something. When do they want to come?"

"I suggested that some time next week would be convenient, but they're pushing to come earlier. If they've found out about the photographs, then if Don Yapley is right, we could be closed down very soon. You'd better tell Norman and Claire. Let's get on with the meeting."

The tea and coffee were made by Alan, but this time Wilkes had given his permission for his team to have something stronger if they wished.

"Listen up everyone. I don't intend to keep you very long today. You've all worked bloody hard for the last two days and even the weather's been against us. We've had a disappointment, that's all. We drew a blank on that line of enquiry, nothing more." He looked across at Alan, who looked even more dejected than the others. "It was a bloody good idea of yours Alan, and one that I totally supported." He took another swallow of his brandy. "The reason I am not bothered about this is because tomorrow at five pm thirty teachers will be waiting outside the education offices, together with the heads of the education and social services departments. Transport has been arranged. Only the departmental heads are aware that this is a police operation, and even they don't know what it is all about. The hall has been booked, so with a bit of luck we can identify these boys and we'll be right back on track."

There was an instant air of rejuvenation and hope amongst the officers. Even hard-bitten old-school detectives can feel despondent, so Mr Wilkes's pep talk had been well timed.

"Thanks for that guv," said Malcolm. He turned to address the team. "Tomorrow we'll start at eight. I want all your ongoing enquiries topped and tailed before we start with the teachers. Now has anyone got anything they want to discuss?"

"Just one thing sir," said Alan. "The professor left you this." Alan passed several pages of computer paper across the table towards Malcolm.

"What is this?" Malcolm was trying to read the information.

"It's the plan of the old and new cemeteries. It shows the approximate layout of the graves and how many people are buried in each plot. I thought your friend the Reverend might find it useful. Do you know there are seven hundred and seventy-seven bodies buried out there?"

Malcolm folded the plan up and placed it in his briefcase. "Thanks Alan. I'll make sure he gets it. See you all in the morning."

When Malcolm arrived at the cottage he was surprised to find it empty, but in a way he was grateful for the peace and quiet. He opened his briefcase and dropped the computer plan of the cemetery on the coffee table. Then he stared at the phone, trying to summon up the courage to phone his wife. He dialled the number, hoping that this time her new man would not answer the phone, but nobody answered. He tried every half an hour until nearly midnight, and then gave up and went to his bedroom and tried to sleep.

In the morning Malcolm woke early. It was barely dawn. He got dressed, grabbed a torch and left the cottage, closing the door quietly behind him as he did so. Then he walked along the drive towards the lane. He needed to clear his head, but his thoughts always returned to his wife and what she might be doing and with whom.

After he had been walking for a few minutes, he found himself standing at the back of the old graveyard looking up at the tower. It seemed to be shrouded in mist, and the air was damp from the previous day's rain. He stopped beside some old headstones and bent down to read the names and dates inscribed on them. He ran his fingers into the grooves that had once borne the names of those interred, like a blind man reading Braille.

"You're right Norman, some of these headstones have been re-carved and even look well cared for," Malcolm murmured to himself. "Did we ever find who was responsible, I wonder." He made a mental note to remind Claire.

He continued along the path towards the tower, then stopped outside the railings and looked up, startled by a pigeon which flapped noisily out of a window high above him. He unlocked the padlock and slipped the chain from the iron gate, then stepped under the blue and white tape. He went up to the door, unlocked it, pushed it back wide against the wall and stepped inside. The early dawn light cast strange shadows around the empty interior, so he switched on his torch. The blood-soaked stone cross was gone, and so were the benches. They had all been removed to the lab for analysis.

He shone his torch towards the stairs, which stretched upwards towards the top of the tower. Then he slowly began to make his way up the old staircase, keeping close to the wall to get the maximum support for his large frame. He stood on a small platform at the top of the stairs and reached above him, then slid back the bolt that fastened the trap door. He pushed it back and hauled himself through the narrow gap onto the flat roof of the tower.

It wasn't that the tower was particularly high, only about forty or fifty feet, but it was enough to see over the trees and across the roofs of nearby houses. The air seemed fresher here somehow, less polluted, or perhaps it was just his imagination. Either way it was very tranquil.

It was then that he noticed that from this vantage point he could see the place where Stephen's body had been buried. The remains of the blue and white tape and the canopy erected to protect the site were clearly visible. Was that significant? They must have known where they were going when they buried him, he reflected. They had gone by the most direct route. You couldn't see the alley from the tower, so they must have known it was there. Were they locals?.

He looked across towards his cottage, but it was obscured by the remains of the old vicarage and its overgrown garden. He paced around the top of the tower deep in thought. You could even see the new graveyard from up there. If they were disturbed by the person who desecrated the grave, did they recognise them, whoever it was? It would be enough to panic them. Why not wait in the tower? Unless they were frightened of being recognised themselves. But perhaps he was giving these perverts too much credit. They hadn't been clever – just bloody lucky.

Malcolm made his way slowly down the stairs, bolting the trap door before he did so. When he reached the bottom, he shone his torch under the stairs onto the pile of broken headstones. He bent down and pulled them a couple of pieces out from under the stairs, wiping away the grey dust that had been left by the scenes of crime officers. He placed the broken pieces together and ran his finger along the grooves and over the faded letters, reading aloud.

"Percy and Ruth Dorking, died August 4th 1665, and

their children Rebecca aged six months, James aged two years, John aged four years, Sarah aged six years. Now at rest. Victims of the plague." Poor buggers. He wondered how many other villagers had died the same way. Whoever had been re-engraving these headstones ought to know. Perhaps it was time they met.

Malcolm was still deep in thought as he slipped the chain around the iron gate. A movement in the bushes behind him made him freeze and he leapt into the bushes, his fists clenched, ready to strike. He started to shout "Come here you bast..." but there was nobody there. He stood silently. Even the birds were strangely still. It must have been his imagination, he thought, but even so, he glanced over his shoulder several times as he made his way back along the narrow path towards the lane. When he reached the lane he looked back towards the tower.

They were right. It was spooky – bloody spooky.

Chapter 20

Malcolm unlocked the door to the murder squad office to be greeted by Norman, who was still dressed in his pyjamas and had obviously just got out of bed. He was still half asleep and looked badly in need of a shave.

"What bloody time do you call this? I've only just woken up," he grumbled.

"I'll tell you what Norman, your wife must have a bloody good sense of humour to wake up each morning and look at you."

"Ha bloody ha. Make yourself useful and put the kettle on. I'll be back in a minute." Norman slung a towel over his shoulder and picked up his toiletries bag.

"It's like being on bloody holiday, only this is a lousy hotel."

When Norman returned, the coffee was waiting for

him. He looked decidedly better and was putting on a clean shirt.

"She looks after you well," said Malcolm, indicating the clean and freshly-ironed shirt.

"Have you rung her yet?" said Norman.

"Nobody could ever accuse you of beating around the bush."

"Well have you?"

"As a matter of fact I rang several times last night, but she never answered. For all I know she's probably living with him now. After I phoned last time."

"How the hell would she know it was you? You never said anything."

"She would have guessed. Probably thought I'd go round and sort him out."

"Would you?" said Norman, looking his old friend straight in the eye.

"I'd like to rip his arm off and beat him over the head with the soggy bit. Poor sod, It's not his fault. He's a lucky man."

"Jesus, I hate it when you start feeling sorry for yourself. Go and see her, sort it out. If you leave it too long she'll think you don't care anyway."

"It's already too late. I've blown it."

A key turned in the door and Alan walked in together with several of the typists, putting an end to their discussion. It never ceased to amaze Malcolm how an office could be empty and silent one minute and the next alive and buzzing, with officers talking on phones, some writing up reports and the typists busy transferring the information onto the Computer.

The kettle was constantly in use. It didn't matter who you were, when you had a drink, everybody had a drink.

Malcolm was with Claire, putting the finishing touches to Operation Identify. Not very original, but to the point. He looked across at Alan, who was finishing off a lengthy report.

"Have you got a moment Alan?"

Alan nodded and followed his boss into the office.

"If it's about the cemetery guv. I honestly thought we would find something."

Malcolm looked at Claire in dismay. "Do you know what he's talking about?"

"Haven't a clue. I just hate him because he's thirty years younger than me."

"I thought it was about yesterday. You know, not finding anything."

"Alan, if I was upset with you you'd would be back in uniform waving your arms about." Sometimes Malcolm felt more like his father than his DI.

"I want you to do a job for me. It will probably mean old fashioned footwork. Going round knocking on doors and talking to people, but it will be good experience."

"I don't mind what it is sir," said Alan, only too

relieved to find he was still on the squad.

"Somebody has been working in the graveyard, re-engraving the headstones. I want you to find him and arrange an interview. Let me know how you get on." Alan was nearly out of the door. "Try the library first, they might be able to help."

Malcolm smiled at Claire. "He's a good lad, a little naive perhaps, but in this job that's an asset. By the way, what did you find out about the young Reverend Winterbourne's activities in Boothstown?"

"You were right. There's nothing positive, nothing written down, but I spoke to a couple of local officers who were on that enquiry. One of them has since retired, but he was very helpful. Apparently Brother Winterbourne, as he was called, used to visit St. Andrews about once a month. He set up a youth club with a swimming section. There's no local baths, so it meant travelling. He used to take the boys in an old minibus and that's when the rumours started. You know, boys being touched up while they were swimming. No one ever complained officially and it was never investigated, but the surprising thing is that he was never even spoken to regarding the disappearance of Dominic Brewer and the murder of Russell Downs. I've read the final report on the enquiry and his name is not mentioned anywhere. The college he used to attend is no longer there. It's now a private hospital."

"You'd think with rumours like that floating around someone would at least speak to him," said Malcolm sarcastically.

"As I said guv, the Reverend Winterbourne, or Brother Winterbourne as he was then, doesn't show anywhere. I've tried every index I can think of. He doesn't even pay tax because he's never earns any money. When he took over this parish he never accepted a salary. He has a private income, which is probably why he got the job in the first place."

"What about that fire? What do we know about that?"

"Only what you know already. I've asked for a file. It should be here this morning. Our Reverend didn't appear to have many friends, although he was close to his brother the MP, who, incidentally, was given a knighthood in the New Year honours list. They have a family home somewhere in Norfolk. It's been in the family for years. They are a very wealthy family."

"Oh. What did you find out about Daniel?"

"No problems there. He was discharged from the army after a sporting accident. Did you know he's deaf in his left ear? He applied for the job along with several other applicants and he got it on merit."

"Thank Christ for that. I'd look a complete prat living with the suspect."

"Especially when you could be back home with your

missus," said Claire without even looking up from the file she was reading.

"Has Norman been talking to you?" Malcolm's voice had an edge to it, but before she could answer, Alan came bursting through the door.

Malcolm swung round to face Alan. "Don't you ever knock? The guvnor might have been in the middle of a personal call to his wife or something."

Malcolm swung back again to face Claire, who just looked at him with a grin on her face. Malcolm knew she was right and whatever rank you are, you can't argue with common sense.

"Sorry sir, I didn't think."

"What are you doing back here anyway? I thought I gave you a job to do."

"Yes sir I know, but I've found him already. I popped in the library a few doors down and there he was. He works there. He's also a local historian and it's him who's been working in the cemetery. He said you can go and see him any time you like."

Claire's grin turned to a broad smile. "That's the trouble with these kids today. They've got no initiative," she said.

The phone rang as she spoke and she picked it up.

"It's for you guv. It's Daniel." She handed the phone to Malcolm and he raised his hand to Alan, indicating for him to stay.

"Hello Dan, I thought you would still be asleep." Malcolm smiled as he spoke.

"Listen Malcolm. The reason I'm phoning is because yesterday I was summoned to see the Bishop. He was furious at police poking around the church grounds. I told him what it was for and that no damage was caused, but it made no difference. He said he was going to contact the Commissioner to complain. He said a strange thing as I was leaving."

"What was that Dan?"

"He said it was very embarrassing for him personally because his predecessor's brother, who as we all know is a Member of Parliament, rings him up and complains that one of his vicars is desecrating the church."

"What did you say to that?"

"Not a lot I could say really, not without telling him that the senior police investigator is staying in the vicarage with me. He also expects me to inform him of all developments that affect the church in any way."

"Thanks Dan. Listen, do you want me to move out? I don't want to drop you in it."

"Don't worry about that. You just find out who did it and don't worry. I won't be telling anybody anything."

"Thanks mate. I appreciate all you've done. See you later."

"No problem. Oh by the way, thanks for the itemised

list of graves. It's very useful, but he got his figures wrong. There are seven hundred and eighty-three bodies, not seven hundred and seventy-seven as the professor says. I expect some of them have sunk too low for his machine to register them."

"How do you remember that figure so clearly?"

"I have to add the details of any person buried in the cemetery in the burial book, which is kept in the church. As you can imagine, some of the books are very old and they are kept in the local museum, but I keep the up to date burial book here in the church and the total is seven hundred and eighty-three bodies, including Ethel, but the main reason I remember it so well is that seven, eight and three were the first three digits of my army number. See you tonight."

Malcolm replaced the receiver. "I think the powers that be are beginning to exert pressure," he said to Claire and then realised that Alan was still in the room. "Could you leave us just for a moment and then we'll go and visit your librarian?"

Alan closed the door behind him and Malcolm explained the conversation he had just had with Daniel. "It would appear that we're beginning to rattle a few cages. Contact Mr Wilkes and tell him what's happened. I'll go with Alan to see our mystery grave prowler."

There was nothing mysterious about Henry Platt.

He was a small man, approaching retirement but with the personality and enthusiasm of someone twice his size and half his age. He showed his guests into his office and sat them down.

"I never tire of talking about history, Inspector, especially local history," he began. "Now how can I help? What aspect of local history are you interested in?"

"I'm interested in St Andrew's church, and in particular the old graveyard. I've noticed that some of the headstones have been restored. I was wondering if you knew who had done it."

"Look no further Inspector, I'm your man. You see, a small village like Etwell is steeped in history and that history needs to be preserved. Did you know, for argument's sake, that on the outskirts of the village they have found Roman remains? They have even found part of the Roman Road which ran from London, or Londinium as it was then..."

"It was the graveyard I was specifically concerned with," interrupted Malcolm.

"Oh, I'm sorry Inspector. You must forgive me. When I start talking about local history I sometimes forget to shut up. Let me see, well there has been a church on that site since the twelfth century. We know that from artefacts found nearby. Church records go back as far as the fifteenth century. As you can see from some of the graves."

"Why is it so important to restore gravestones?" enquired Alan.

"A very good question, young man. You see a cemetery as old as this is an integral part of the village. Out there is our history. Did you know, for example, that a detachment of soldiers from Charles the First's personal bodyguard stopped to water their horses in the very pond that you have just walked past to get here?"

"That's amazing," said Alan who was becoming engrossed.

"That's not all. The senior ranking officer – I think he was a captain, if I remember rightly – was kicked in the head by his own horse and killed instantly, and he's buried in St Andrew's without any indication as to his position. You see, the villagers were afraid of reprisals from the Roundheads. There is also a headstone that has a sculpture of the deceased on it. It's nearly three hundred years old. Of course, nowadays we sometimes have photographs of our loved ones on their graves."

"That's very interesting, Mr Platt," said Malcolm. "What did the Reverend Winterbourne think about you working in his graveyard?"

"Don't talk to me about that man. Called himself a Christian! He went berserk when I was working on a headstone. He physically threw me out of the churchyard, it was most embarrassing. I could not believe a vicar would ever do such a thing. He was shouting and screaming about desecration. I am not a churchgoer Inspector, though I support everyone's right to worship or not as they wish, but how on earth that man ever became a member of the clergy defies belief."

"You didn't like him very much then," smiled Alan.

"That is an understatement," Mr Platt then realised he was being sent up and smiled back. "I still go there though, to continue my research and restoration."

"Have you ever been in the old tower?"

"Yes, several times, but not for years. That was something else that that so-called Christian decreed. He decided that the old church tower was unsafe and no one was to enter. It was he who had the iron railings erected to stop anyone getting in, and he held the only key. Let me tell you Inspector, that tower has stood for five hundred years and it's good for another five hundred. It was just sheer bloody-mindedness on his part."

"What happened to the other soldiers?" asked Alan. "You know, when their Captain was killed. Did they stay in Etwell?"

"No, they went on to fight a big battle at Dorking, not far from here as you know, and they were all killed."

"I came across a broken headstone with the name of Dorking on it inside the tower," said Malcolm.

"Oh, you mean Percy and Ruth and their four

children. That was a part of local history that this village would sooner forget, but history has a nasty habit of never going away."

"Why, what happened to them?" enquired Alan. He was beginning to annoy Malcolm with questions that appeared to have nothing to do with the matter in hand.

"They died of the plague and they're buried in the old graveyard," said Malcolm in a matter of fact sort of way.

"Well, you're partly right, Inspector. They did die of the plague, but they're not buried in the cemetery. Do you know they walked all the way from London to escape the plague? In those days, young man, it was a dangerous journey and very few people ever attempted it, but Percy and Ruth were trying to save their children. When they arrived on the outskirts of the parish they had already been contaminated and the villagers wouldn't let them in. They wouldn't even give them any food or water, such was the fear in people's minds. The Dorking family died of starvation and the plague. When their remains were gathered up for burial they were placed in a corner of the old graveyard, but the villagers were so afraid they refused even to go to church for fear of catching the disease, so the remains were dug up late at night and re-interred in an unmarked grave in the gardens of the vicarage. I mean the old vicarage of course, the one that was burnt down and took the life of

Reverend Winterbourne."

"So why is the headstone in the tower?"

"Well, as I said, they were buried it in an unmarked grave, but not till several years later. The vicar of the day paid from his own pocket to have a proper headstone erected."

"I still don't understand," persisted Alan, much to the annoyance of his boss

"Well in 1998, 321 years after their deaths, the good people of this parish finally made amends. A beautiful stone vault was commissioned and paid for by the villagers and Percy and Ruth, together with their four children, were finally laid to rest. It made all the papers at the time, lots of dignitaries, you know the sort of thing."

"So where is the grave now? I don't remember seeing any large vault in the graveyard," insisted Alan.

"It's where it was before, in the garden of the old vicarage."

"You mean there's six bodies buried in the back garden of that burnt-down house?"

Malcolm was now showing a great deal of interest at this latest news and he looked across at Alan, who also realised its significance.

"You have been very helpful and most interesting Mr Platt," said Malcolm.

"Any time, Inspector."

The three men stood up and Mr Platt opened the door for his guests.

"One more thing, Mr Platt. When was the last time you were in the graveyard?"

"About two or three weeks ago. I can check my diary if it's important."

"No, not at all Mr Platt. Have you ever met the new vicar?"

"I've seen him many times around the village of course and I'm told he is a very nice chap, but I'm afraid I didn't ask his permission either. I didn't want to run the risk of being banned."

"You speak to him. I think you'll like him."

Once outside the library, Malcolm stopped for a moment to collect his thoughts.

"How do you fancy a spot of burglary, Alan?" he said.

They returned to the station to collect a car and drove directly to the cottage, but this time Malcolm parked the car outside the Old Vicarage. The garden gate was hardly visible among the dense foliage.

"We're going to need a machete to hack our way through this lot," said Alan. He kicked at the gate, hoping to free it from the bushes' stranglehold and it crumbled in front of him. Only the hinges were left hanging from what remained of the post.

"You're not obliged to say anything, but," said

Malcolm with a grin.

"Sorry sir, it came off in my hand."

Alan pushed his way through the undergrowth along what had once been a path. He snagged his tie on a bush and yanked it free, only to find his trousers caught on more thorny bushes.

"We're not exactly dressed for this sort of thing, are we sir?"

"Not to worry. Think of the team's reaction when you tell them you've cracked the case."

If Alan had turned round, he would have seen the smile on his boss's face. He kept close to him, protecting himself from the brambles that seemed determined to ruin his nice suit.

The path divided into two and ran either side of the once glorious house.

"You go that way and I'll meet you at the back," said Malcolm. He directed Alan to follow what was left of the path to the right of the house, while Malcolm struggled around to the left. When he neared the back of the house, he stopped to look more clearly at the burnt-out shell. The back of the house was badly damaged. A large section of wall had crashed into what was left of the conservatory. The roof, or what was left of it, lay precariously on the first floor. The remains of a conservatory which must once have overlooked the garden were now choked with weeds and bushes as Mother Nature continued her relentless invasion.

Malcolm looked towards the rear garden. It was dense, but you could still make out the edges of the once-manicured lawns. The fruit trees were beginning to blossom, but they were in desperate need of attention.

"Where do we start looking?" called Alan from the other side of the garden.

"I don't like to tell you Alan, but when you're committing burglary a prime requisite is to be quiet," Malcolm said through clenched teeth.

"Sorry," came the whispered reply.

Malcolm found part of a spade and used the blade to cut his way through the tangled mass that had once been the garden. He saw how the high walls must have protected it from nosy neighbours. He rebuked himself; it had never crossed his mind, even when staying next door, to include this old burnt-out shell in the searches. He was beginning to think he should have got a search team in to find the crypt, especially as he kept losing his shoe in deep mud.

It was when he was bending down to retrieve it for the second time that he saw a vertical grey stone surface. The vault was almost hidden from view, but on looking more closely he could make out the outline. It was about five feet high, twelve feet long and six feet wide. He began pulling the weeds from the memorial stone.

"Percy and Ruth Dorking and their four children

Rebecca, James, John, Sarah - Victims of the Plague. Died August 4th 1665 - Finally laid to rest 12th September 1988," he read.

"Alan, over here" he called quietly.

Alan was closer than he thought and appeared through the bushes almost at once. Without speaking they both started pulling away the ferns and bushes that surrounded the tomb.

"I think I've found the entrance sir," said Alan quietly.

Malcolm came round to join him. Two steps led down to the base of the crypt and what had once been an entrance.

"This must be it, but there's no door." Alan's voice was quiet, even reverential.

"No reason why there should be, after all they weren't expecting any other members of the family to be buried here. The entrance would have been sealed."

"If the family were finally laid to rest, as it says here on 12th September 1988, that's four days after Derek went missing. So he could easily be inside," said Alan.

"And if he is, it's a racing certainty that the gravedigger, Bill Schneider and possibly Winterbourne himself knew all about it"

"I think we might have cracked this, you know. Let's get back to the office. I'd like to talk to our professor again before I get a warrant."

The two made their way back along the path towards

the car.

"What are you doing? Stand still!" a voice boomed at them from the direction of the lane. They looked round to see Constable Vincent Bradley on the path in front of them.

"Oh, it's you sir," he said. "I was just passing and I noticed that some clown had smashed the gate down. I'm afraid I didn't recognise your car. This *is* your car, I take it?"

"Yes it is. It's Vince Bradley isn't it?" said Malcolm, playing for time.

"That's right sir, but can I ask what you're doing here?" The officer was sweating slightly and looked very tense.

"Young Sherlock here was convinced he heard someone moving about in the garden. Needless to say he was wrong, but it was worth the effort." Malcolm held out his hands and displayed his mud-covered trousers and shoes.

"I'm sorry sir, I was sure I heard something," said Alan, putting on a shame-faced look as he went along with his boss's story.

"Probably a fox or a badger. These kids, give 'em a warrant card and they think everybody they meet is a villain. Can't switch off for a moment. Like dogs on heat."

"You're right there, Vince."

Constable Bradley watched as they drove down the lane until they were out of out of sight, and then he climbed back over the fence and disappeared into the garden.

They arrived back in the office and were met by Chief Superintendent Wilkes.

"What have you been doing to upset the Bishop then?" he said.

"They don't waste any time, do they?"

"Don't worry Malcolm. If anybody asks, you've had a bollocking from me for messing about in the Bishop's graveyard."

"Well, you'd better give me another one because I'm just about to do the same thing in his garden, on a smaller scale, and I think it's time we let everyone know what's really going on." Wilkes nodded his agreement.

"OK everyone, gather round, I've got something to tell you."

Malcolm told his team everything that had happened, including his meeting with Don Yapley and the fact that both Winterbourne brothers were suspects, together with any number of high-ranking persons who might come to light.

"So you now understand the need for absolute secrecy. I want to get into these people before they have a chance to close us down. A great deal is going to depend on the identification of these boys and whether or not our professor can find anything in the burial vault."

"What's your plan of action? Search warrant>" enquired Wilkes.

"Not just yet. Claire, Can you see if you can get hold of Professor Kennard? I don't care what you do. Offer him a chauffeur-driven car there and back, offer to put him and his assistant up in a honeymoon hotel, offer him anything just get him here. Tell him the size of it, just in case that makes a difference."

Claire disappeared into the small office and started dialling.

"Does anyone know how we're doing with the local pervs?" asked Wilkes.

"They've all been turned over guv, negative result."

"I didn't expect to have a result. Our suspects are much closer to home."

Malcolm watched as Claire made her phone call to Matthew Kennard. She was obviously talking to someone, because he could see her smiling. At last she replaced the receiver and came back into the office.

"He's on his way. He'll be here about two o'clock and he'll meet you at the cottage. He's going to use the handheld machine. He reckons it will work OK."

"That's great," said Malcolm. He turned to Wilkes.

"Governor, if the professor finds something, would you mind getting the warrant? Only the muppets on the bench will take more notice of you."

"No problem. I'll be on the end of a phone."

"Oh guv, that file on the fire investigation finally turned up," said Claire. "It makes interesting reading. It's on your desk."

Malcolm went into the office and opened the file. The name of Andrew Summers, Chief Fire Investigator, appeared several times in the report.

"If you want me I'll be at Andrew Summers' house," he said. "You can contact me on my mobile. Tell Norman and Alan to meet me at the cottage at one-thirty."

Chapter 21

"Come on in Malcolm, it's nice to see you again."

"I hope I'm not disturbing you Andrew, only I wanted to talk to you about the fire at the vicarage and this report of yours."

"I was wondering if you would want to speak to me about that, given what's happened just lately."

Andrew followed his guest into the lounge and Malcolm opened the file and laid it on the table between them.

"Sorry about the mess. I just don't seem to have the time any more. Actually that's not true. I just don't have the inclination any more. Well, how can I help you?"

"Did you ever read the finished report on the vicarage fire?"

"Of course I did, I wrote most of it. As you can see

from the report, we worked very closely with your boys. I have to say they were very professional and thorough, although we did have our differences."

"What do you mean exactly?"

"Oh, I don't just mean the police. No, we were evenly divided. I and the senior police investigator both agreed that it could have been a possible murder scene."

"What?"

"Wait a minute Malcolm, don't jump to the wrong conclusions, there was no smoking gun or anything like that. The only reason we even considered that was because there was no positive identification, or at least none that we thought was very satisfactory."

"Are you telling me that nobody ever identified the body?"

"Well as I said, not to my satisfaction, and certainly not to the satisfaction or your senior police chap. I wish I could remember his name. You see when the building caught fire, several large beams fell on the Reverend Winterbourne, smashing his skull and jaw. The intense heat then reduced the bone structure to virtual powder."

"So what you're saying is, that there was no orthodontic identification?"

"You're catching on fast."

"So how was he identified?"

"Quite frankly, the remains would have fitted nicely into a large manila envelope, but his brother, you know the MP, identified a gold ring and cross that were found near the body as belonging to his brother."

"So it could have been anybody." Malcolm's mind was racing.

"And another thing, the man who they thought was trying to save him – what was his name, German sounding – Schneider, that was it. Well, if he was trying to save the vicar, he didn't try very hard. His body was found outside the front door." He could see the puzzled look on Malcolm's face. "The door was open."

"How can you be so sure of that?"

"Let me explain. The seat of the fire was at the rear of the house. The vicar's body, or what was supposed to be the vicar's body, was found on the ground floor, perhaps thirty to thirty-five feet from the front door. Now although the front of the house was badly damaged, It didn't melt the locks or bolts on the front door and they were all in the unlocked position. So the front door was unlocked."

"Well if that's the case why did he try to get into the house, when he could have just called the brigade? How did he die, anyway?"

"Well that's another thing. You see the doctors said it was due to a crack on the head from a fallen beam."

"Those beams get everywhere."

"Don't they just? But the coroner's report says he

died of smoke inhalation."

"Is that possible?"

"Yes, anything's possible, but to die of smoke inhalation outside the house is unlikely."

"Answer me one thing Andrew. Why is it that what you've just told me doesn't appear in your report?"

"Don't be daft, it does. I signed the completed report myself before it was filed. Let me see." He scanned the file. "Hang on! That's my signature, but it's not my report. I promise you, I put everything in that report that I've just told you, and more."

"Steady on, I believe you."

"What's going on? Why should anyone want to change my report?"

"I honestly don't know at the moment, but after what you've just told me I've a pretty good idea."

"You mean it's a cover up? But why? You're not suggesting that the vicar is still alive, are you?" Andrew's face suddenly lit up. "You think he's got something to do with this murdered boy, don't you?"

"As I said, I honestly don't know, but I'm damn well going to find out. There are just too many unanswered questions. Like why didn't the insurance company pay up? After all, this report just says it was a nasty accident. I think they concluded it was a piece of hot coal landing on the carpet that started the fire."

"I might be able to answer the question about the

insurance company. You see within hours of the fire, loss adjusters were on the site. After all, it was a historic listed building. But they knew we were divided in our opinion not only on how the fire started but on the cause of death."

"That may explain why the Church didn't ask for compensation. They knew the insurance company would conduct their own investigation, and that might prove very awkward." Malcolm was beginning to feel a buzz.

"If this is a cover up, it must involve people at the very highest level, fire service, the police."

"And the Church, and what's more, his brother," said Malcolm.

"If you're right about the vicar, who's buried in the grave? If it's not Joseph Winterbourne, who is it?"

"I don't know, but like I said I'm sure as hell going to find out. Now I must go, I've got an important meeting."

"If there's anything I can do you only have to ask."

Malcolm was about to reply when Andrew interrupted him. "I know what you're going to say, Malcolm. I might be retired, but I'm not in my dotage. I know how to keep secrets."

"Actually I wasn't going to say that at all. I was going to ask you to do me a favour. You might not get too much thanks for it."

"Just name it."

"Will you ring June at the cottage? I want to make

sure she is out of the way. If she answers, tell her your popping round to see her. I want her in the cottage for the next hour or so."

Andrew looked at his guest very closely. He scanned his face for any sign that might give him a clue, and then it dawned on him.

"You know where her brother is, don't you? You've found his body."

"Andrew, I was convinced that I would find Derek in the graveyard, but I was wrong. I could be wrong again. After what happened last time, I just don't want to give her any false hope."

"Consider it done. I'll ring her now."

Andrew dialled the number. He let it ring several times.

"There's no reply."

"That's good enough for me," replied Malcolm.

"I hope you find him, for June's sake."

The two men shook hands firmly, then Andrew watched Malcolm climb into his car and disappear.

Malcolm drove directly to the cottage. He was grateful that Dan's Hillman was not there. Hopefully that meant he was busy on parish business and it was less likely that June was at home.

He opened the cottage door and called out just in case, but the place was empty. He started to think. If this was a cover up... but on such a scale! How high did it go, and who was involved? Special Branch, MI5? The Commissioner's task force? The task force had been set up to investigate serious and potentially embarrassing situations, from corruption in high places to MPs losing their House of Commons security passes in brothels.

Malcolm walked up the driveway towards the lane. When he reached the gate he closed it behind him and stood for a moment looking across the lane towards the church and the old flint wall that surrounded it and the cemetery. Was it really possible that something so evil could have happened in such a peaceful place?

Part of Malcolm's question was about to be answered, because just then Professor Kennard's Audi turned the corner and he walked over to meet him.

"Did you have a good journey Matthew? No Rachel today?"

"I thought it was better she didn't come this time, and the journey was fine, thank you very much," said Matthew tersely.

"Is there a problem? Is it something we've done?"

"Not unless you've got powerful friends at the university."

"I don't understand. What's happened?"

"I got a call from the Dean this morning. It seems his mate the Bishop was really pissed off at me carrying out research in his churchyard. Perhaps he's got a point, I don't know, but when they start threatening to take away my research grant, they can stuff it."

"What does that mean exactly? Are you out of a job?"

"Don't be daft. I've got all the right qualifications except diplomacy. My old man always said I was too bloody minded by half."

"I'm sorry. I seem to have dropped you right in it."

"I was really pissed off when the Dean threatened me. That's why I'm here." He climbed out of his car and slammed the door behind him. He was resplendent in an evening dress suit complete with bow tie.

"If I'd known you were that annoyed, I would have dressed up myself," said Malcolm.

Matthew pulled a pair of overalls from the back seat and put them on. "Don't worry, I haven't got dressed up on your account. I'm giving a talk at Guildford University. I might even ask them for a job. You know this investigation of yours must be serious to involve the Dean, he normally keeps a low profile, but I still don't like being leaned on or threatened. They should have taken my old man's advice."

"What was that?"

"Do your bloody homework first. If they think they're going to push me around they've got another think coming."

"Have you done this sort of thing before? I mean helping the police."

"My dear old mate, I and my team have not only helped

just about every police force in this country but also in Egypt, Israel and Russia during the Chernobyl disaster and several other countries, including the States. That's why I'm so pissed off over what's happened. Now show me where this tomb is."

It was now Malcolm's turn to lead the way through the thorny bushes.

"Where the bloody hell is everyone? They should have been here by now," Malcolm muttered between clenched teeth. Matthew followed him around to the back of the house and arrived at the tomb.

"Well this won't take long. This is the only one, isn't it?" Matthew didn't wait for a reply. He just handed Malcolm what looked like a large frying pan with leads coming out of the handle.

"Just wait till I plug it in to the laptop and then start on the other side. Hold it as close to the surface as possible without touching it. I then want you to walk slowly around the tomb."

Malcolm did as he was instructed.

"That's great. Now follow the same procedure across the top. Yeah that's it, bloody marvellous. Won't be long now."

Malcolm held the pan-like object over the top of the tomb. He ran it backwards and forwards, covering every inch of its surface.

"That's wonderful. You see, didn't take long."

"Is that it, have you finished?"

Professor Kennard was busy examining his computer. "Yeah, that's it Malcolm. As you know from the inscription on the tomb it's a multiple gravesite, but with one difference, there are at least seven sets of skeletal remains inside. I'm not too sure about this area here, you see." Matthew showed Malcolm the graph. Even to his untrained eye, it clearly showed seven shaded areas and a less shaded area in the centre of the tomb.

"It might even be a sort of echo. It sometimes happens when bodies have been buried close together. I hope it's what you want. I'm out of here."

"Thanks for everything Matthew, and don't forget, if you ever need a hand with your homework, give me a ring."

The two men shook hands warmly and Malcolm watched as he disappeared through the bushes. Malcolm's thoughts returned to more mundane matters. Where the bloody hell were the team? They were told to be here forty minutes ago. He took his mobile phone from his pocket and dialled.

"Is that you Claire? Where the hell is everyone?"

"I think you'd better come in, guv."

"Trouble?"

"You could say that."

"I'll be right there."

Malcolm drove directly to the office. He didn't drive very fast, as he wanted to consider all his options. Whatever the problem was, he was about to find out.

The door to his murder squad office was ajar. He pushed it back and stood in the doorway. All his team were sitting in silence around the table as he entered.

"So glad you could find the time to join us, Inspector."

Deputy Assistant Kendrick was small in stature for a policeman. As a graduate entrant he had risen through the ranks very quickly and had been largely protected from the day-to-day dangers of policing. Instead he had concentrated on the managerial side of police work. Malcolm always referred to his type as 'theoretical policemen'.

"Now that you're all here, I have something to say that concerns each and every one of you, and I have no intention of repeating myself."

"Pompous little shit," Malcolm muttered to himself.

"I have received the strongest possible complaint from the Bishop."

"Which bishop is that sir?" said Norman, with all the sarcasm he could muster."

"The Bishop of London. I presume you do know who I'm talking about."

Norman shook his head. "Never found much use for them myself."

"Yes, I can well believe that. Now where was I? I

understand, Chief Superintendent, that you have ridden roughshod over consecrated ground. I'm sure you know what I mean."

"I take full responsibility for the actions of all my officers, sir, and I can assure you that the investigation carried out in the graveyard was necessary and there was no damage caused to any property," said Wilkes.

"I'm glad to hear it. And did you actually find whatever it was you were looking for?"

"No sir, and all enquiries of that nature have finished. Isn't that right Inspector?"

"Absolutely right sir," said Malcolm. "We're continuing to question all known paedophiles and sex offenders in the area and widening the house to house enquiries."

DAC Kendrick's high-handed approach seemed to soften slightly, but only slightly.

"I don't mean to be rude, but you just don't appreciate the ramifications of your actions, Inspector. As for you, Chief Superintendent, we are all only too well aware that you are approaching your retirement. I would have thought ending it with a good result would have been uppermost in your mind. Instead you have allowed this investigation to get completely out of control. Are you hearing me, Mr Wilkes?"

"I'm retiring sir, not retarded, and yes I do hear you,"

replied Wilkes.

"I'm glad to hear it. I want you all to be quite clear about one thing. If there's repetition of this sort in that graveyard, you will all be replaced, and I do mean all. Do I make myself clear?"

"I think my officers can grasp the rudiments of the English language." Mr Wilkes rose from his chair to face the DAC. "Does this mean we won't have the pleasure of Sir Henry Winterbourne's company next week, and of course your good self?"

"We'll be here, Chief Superintendent." DAC Kendrick picked up his cap, gloves and swagger stick and walked towards the door. "One more thing, Inspector. Get these window screens taken down at once. It looks more like a cinema than a murder squad office. And I won't have office doors locked, is that clear? It creates a fire hazard. Suppose someone wanted to get in?"

"You're quite right sir."

DAC Kendrick left the office and smiled to himself as he walked back to his car. He was well aware of the contempt they felt for him, and somehow it made him feel much happier.

The room remained in silence until Malcolm spoke.

"Sir, before we go any further, I must bring you up to speed with what's happened this morning, and I think all the team should be aware of what's going on."

"I agree Malcolm. Lock the door, somebody. It

remains locked until this investigation is over, and those screens stay where they are as well."

Malcolm recounted the events of the past few hours, the threat made to the Professor and his pal Daniel and now a visit from the DAC. But there was a great sense of excitement when he told them what Professor Kennard had found in the vault.

"According to the Professor there are at least seven bodies in that vault. Six can be accounted for, but the other, I believe, is Derek Walsh. The Dorking family were re-interred on the 12th September 1988, that's just a few days after Derek Walsh went missing. Which implicates Bill Schneider and both the Winterbourne brothers. And our old mate the Bishop conducted the service."

"Is that the same Bishop who's kicking his toys around?" said Norman.

"One and the same."

"So what about your theory that the vicar is still alive? If that's the case, who's buried in his place, and who really died in that fire?" asked one of the team.

"Norman, ring missing persons and check the date of the fire against all persons who went missing at the same time." Malcolm tossed the file on the fire investigation across the table. "You never know, we might strike lucky."

Norman disappeared into the small office away from

the chatter.

"Claire, are we all set for this evening?"

"Yes guv. Of all the schools representatives that have been invited, only three have said they won't be there. They all have legitimate reasons and they're sending replacements, and most of them have been at their respective schools for more than ten years. So if these boys turn out to be local, we should be able to identify them."

"Excellent work. Guvnor," said Malcolm, turning to Mr Wilkes, "will you arrange for a warrant, first thing in the morning to search the vault? We'll also need the Coroner to attend the scene. Will you arrange that, Claire?"

"Leave it to me."

"When we open that tomb, I want the forensic team and the photographers standing by. I don't want to be waiting all day. I want the area sealed off tight. Can you sort that out Alan? I don't want to give anybody time to react, especially the press. If we get a result with identifying these boys, I want to move fast."

"You know that this story will break eventually and there will be a lot of shit flying around, I hope we are all prepared for it," said Wilkes.

"In my case only the depth of shit varies," said Claire.

"If you get any problems at all from the press or the big house, give them to me. I'll be at home. Good night all and watch your backs." He left the room.

"Any luck with missing persons?" Malcolm shouted at Norman, who was sitting with the phone against one ear and his finger plugged into the other, trying to listen. "Thanks, that's great," he said, and replaced the receiver. "I think this is what you're after, boss."

"Quiet everyone. Go on Norman."

"Trevor Neading, aged 26. Disappeared on the same day as the fire and never seen again. He lived with his parents in Surbiton."

"That's just down the road. Do we know if they still live there? Someone do a voters check with the local station."

"No need, boss. The Neadings still live there. They write or phone every few months or so, to see if there's any news. The chap I was just speaking to has spoken to them two or three times on the phone and he reckons they're a sweet old couple. Oh there's one more thing. You'll never guess what Trevor did for a living."

"Come on, what was it?" said Malcolm impatiently. He had known his friend for too long not to recognise that glint in his eye.

"He was a parliamentary researcher at the House of Commons."

"Yes!" Malcolm hit the table with his clenched fist.

"Right Norman, you come with me. The rest of you finish up your enquiries. We'll just make it back in time for our teachers. Claire, sorry to lumber you but in the event that the boys are identified I want interview teams set up and ready to go at a moment's notice."

They pulled up outside the house of Mr and Mrs Neading a short while later. It was a smart middle terrace Victorian property. Its small, neat flowerbeds spilled over onto the path that ran up to the front door, which unlike similar houses in the street, still retained the original stained glass panel in the front door.

Malcolm rapped on the brass knocker and they took out their warrant cards ready for inspection. An elderly man opened the door.

"Good afternoon sir. I'm Detective Inspector Cammock and this is my colleague, Detective Constable Harris. It is Mr Neading, isn't it?"

"Yes it is. What's happened?"

"Nothing at all, Mr Neading. We would just like to ask you a few questions about your son, if we may."

The door was pulled further back by unseen hands and Mrs Neading stood alongside her husband. She was a small woman and she appeared nervous.

"Have you found him, Inspector? Have you any news?"

"I'm sorry Mrs Neading, I don't mean to distress you. It's just that we're updating all our information on missing persons and following certain lines of enquiry, but I mustn't raise your hopes. I do hope you understand."

"But what lines of enquiry, Inspector? It must be something important." Mrs Neading became quite agitated.

"Now come on mother, we're forgetting our manners," said Mr Neading. "Come in Inspector. You go and make the tea, mother."

Malcolm was grateful for the intervention of Mr Neading, who showed them into the lounge while Mrs Neading prepared some refreshment. The room was neat and tidy, but there was something else about it. Malcolm couldn't quite put his finger on it until it suddenly occurred to him that all the photographs that adorned the walls and mantelpiece were of the family and they all included Trevor. They seemed to trace his short life from baby, infant and child to schoolboy and into adulthood, and there they stopped.

"There we are Inspector, that didn't take long." Mrs Neading placed the tray of tea and homemade cakes on a small table in front of them and then sat next to her husband and started pouring the tea. Mr Neading passed around the plates and large slices of jam sponge topped with icing.

"What a lovely spread. I'm surprised you two have both stayed so slim," said Malcolm as he took a bite from the sponge.

"You look like a man who appreciates home cooking.

Does your wife cook?"

"Oh yes, she's a great cook. Not as good as this, mark you, but don't tell her that."

It was ironic that this was the first time he had ever commented on his wife's cooking. It was true, she was a good cook, but that was the least part of her he was missing right now.

"I've had a lot more practice than your young wife, Inspector." She smiled at him. "I'm sorry I was a little over anxious before."

"Not at all Mrs Neading. It's very understandable. You hear nothing for years and then two policemen turn up on your doorstep asking about your son."

"We'll help you all we can, won't we mother?" Mr Neading held his wife's hand and she squeezed it in response.

"As I said, we're following up on several lines of enquiries and at the same time updating our information."

"But we gave the police all the information we had at the time. After all this time, are you sure you still can't tell us anything about Trevor?" Mrs Neading was almost pleading with them.

"I wish we could be the bearer of good news, but sadly It's just as the Inspector says. We don't mean to upset you," said Norman. He was now standing by the mantelpiece looking at all the photographs.

"It doesn't matter what the reason is, does it mother? If we can help in any way."

"We were very proud of our son, Inspector. He was our only child. We tried for a long time. I lost my first two at birth, stillborn. We were blessed with Trevor, weren't we?" She paused for a moment and Malcolm saw Mr Neading squeeze her hand. "I had him late in life you see. I was nearly forty-two."

"Come on now mother. I'm sure the Inspector doesn't want to listen to us blabber on about our troubles."

"On the contrary, Mr Neading," said Malcolm. "Please go on, Mrs Neading."

"I'm sorry Inspector. You see, we have never given up hope that one day Trevor will walk in through that door."

"Have you kept his room ready for him?" asked Norman. He wasn't being insensitive; he knew from years of experience that it was very common for people in the Neadings' position to do just that.

"I suppose you think we're very silly, but you're right, we have kept his room just as Trevor left it."

"I don't think that's silly at all. I would probably do the same thing. It's a way of remembering. Keeping them alive in your thoughts."

"You really do understand, Inspector."

"I try Mrs Neading, but fortunately but I've never been in your position and I hope I never am. Now tell me some more about Trevor."

Malcolm offered his cup for a refill and gladly took another slice of cake that was offered. At the same time he was wondering how he would react if one of his children disappeared off the face of the earth – those same children who by now must be asking, "When is daddy coming back?"

"He was so good looking and intelligent." Mrs Neading smiled. "I suppose all parents would say that about their children, wouldn't they?"

"You're so right. What my boys know about computers leaves me standing," said Malcolm.

"He passed all his A levels, and with good grades." She rose and reached for a photograph on the mantelpiece. "This was taken on his first day at Oxford. We were so proud, weren't we father? He did so well. He got an honours degree in Law."

"But his real love was politics."

"Oh yes. We always thought that one day he would be an MP."

"That's quite an achievement. You must have been very proud of him," remarked Norman.

"To be honest, we were a little disappointed. After all that effort, he threw it all up to work as a researcher in the Houses of Parliament, but he was happy and that's all that matters. He talked of nothing else." Mrs Neading was smiling as she spoke. She appeared to be reliving every moment she had spent with her son.

"When Trevor was at university, he got involved in all sorts of political groups, that's what got him started."

"Did he work for anyone in particular?"

"Well to start with he was just a run around boy, but then Sir Henry invited him to join his staff. Well! You can imagine Trevor was overjoyed."

"I'm sorry Mrs Neading, excuse my ignorance. Sir Henry who?" Malcolm said, feigning ignorance.

"Sir Henry Winterbourne, Inspector. The Home Secretary. He was so helpful and charming to us when Trevor disappeared. I think he pulled a few strings," Mrs Neading dropped her voice, as though she thought someone might be listening.

"Does he still keep in touch?" said Norman, as he helped himself to another piece of cake.

"Sir Henry used to call round quite often, every few months or so. To see how we were."

"But he hasn't been round for some time, mother."

"That's because he's so busy, but he did ring a few days ago."

Malcolm and Norman were not the only ones to be startled at this information.

"You didn't tell me that mother. What did he want?" If Mr Neading was annoyed at this revelation, he didn't show it.

"He only rang to see how we were. I didn't want you

getting upset, especially after what happened to that young boy. The world is a very wicked place Inspector, isn't it?"

"It's not the world, mother. It's the people in it."

"Did you ever meet Sir Henry's family?" asked Malcolm, changing the subject.

"Never. He only ever came to the house."

"Hold on father, you're forgetting that time Trevor took us to Sir Henry's house in Norfolk. You know, when he was re-elected. When was it?"

"You're right, fancy me forgetting that. It was a long time ago and none of his family were there. I think they're separated."

"Isn't it sad Inspector, that so many couples split up, or am I just old fashioned?"

"I think it's probably the pressure of the job. It can drive people apart." Norman looked meaningfully at his friend. "Was Trevor a religious man."

"That's a strange question to ask. What on earth have his religious beliefs got to do with him disappearing?"

"Nothing at all, Mrs Neading. We're just exploring every avenue."

"Inspector, my son was twenty-six when he disappeared from our life. The only thing that has kept us going is our belief in God. Trevor was brought up a Christian, but when he started working at the Houses of Parliament we saw a lot less of him. He very often stayed in town or at Sir Henry's house in Norfolk, so whether he was attending church regularly, I'm afraid we can't help you."

"You've both been very helpful. Would it be possible to see Trevor's room?" asked Malcolm sympathetically.

"Of course Inspector. Follow me. I was wondering when you were going to ask." She led Malcolm upstairs to the rear bedroom. "This is it Inspector. Your colleague was right. It's exactly as Trevor left it."

Mrs Neading started to cry, trying to hide her tears in a handkerchief. Malcolm placed a comforting arm on her shoulder.

"It's not knowing that really hurts. I don't care if the press do come round. If they can help find our son..."

"What have the press got to do with it?" Malcolm spoke in a matter of fact sort of way, as though he wasn't really interested.

"Sir Henry told me when he phoned the other day that the gutter press, as he calls them, might want to drag over old coals and that I should not let them in or speak to them because it would just be too upsetting."

"What sort of trouble, did he say?"

"No not exactly, but he said Trevor was not here to defend himself so he was going to deal with everything."

"Trevor didn't have any dark secrets, did he?" laughed Malcolm.

"Of course not, but Sir Henry said if anyone came

round I was to inform him straight away."

Malcolm closed the door behind him and followed Mrs Neading back to the lounge, where Mr Needing was showing Norman a photograph album.

"You ought to look at these, boss, they're really interesting," said Norman, looking his boss straight in the eye. "Mr Neading is going to let us borrow it for a while."

"Thank you. We'll take good care of it and return it as soon as possible," said Malcolm.

"If you think it will help, Inspector."

They all shook hands and Mr Needing followed them out to the front gate. He held out his hand to Malcolm once again and gripped it tightly. He spoke directly and to the point, out of earshot of his beloved wife.

"Inspector, I know my son is probably dead, but my wife has never come to terms with that. If during the course of your investigation you find something out, even if you can't prove anything, will you come and tell us? We can't go on forever like we are now."

Malcolm felt strangely ashamed at having misled such a charming and loving couple.

"Mr Neading, as soon as I have any information at all I will come and tell you personally, and that's a promise."

It was several minutes into the car journey before either of them spoke.

"What a lovely couple," said Malcolm. "They don't deserve any of this. They have no idea what goes on around them."

"Perhaps they're the lucky ones," replied Norman.

"What was so interesting about those photographs?"

Norman opened the album that had been resting on his lap.

"This." He held the photograph up in front of Malcolm so he could see it and still drive the car. It was a picture of Trevor Neading between two older men. One was Sir Henry, and the other was a smartly-dressed man wearing a clerical collar.

Malcolm pulled the car into the kerb and stopped. He took the photograph and examined it.

"Is that the Winterbourne brothers with Trevor? So the vicar knew Trevor as well."

"It's what's written on the back that's interesting, boss."

Malcolm turned the photo over and read, *To Trevor. Many Thanks. Love Henry.*

"That's a very affectionate way to treat your staff."

"Wait till you see this one." Norman handed another photograph to Malcolm.

"The bastards," was all Malcolm said. He started the car and headed back to the office.

It was a photograph they had both seen before. Don Yapley had shown it to them, only then it had been part of a book. It was a photograph of two men dressed in monks' robes; Maurice Flowers and the Reverend Winterbourne. The message on the back was equally affectionate.

Thanks for all you help. Love Maurice.

Maurice Flower – the Chief Constable of Greater Manchester Police.

Chapter 22

The office seemed to come alive when Malcolm and Norman told them what they had just discovered from Mr and Mrs Neading.

"If that's the case guvnor, this reverend could still be alive and kicking. I take it he has just become our number one suspect," said one of the officers seated round the table.

"Not forgetting the Chief Constable, our Member of Parliament and former Home Secretary would you believe, and possibly the Bishop of London," said another.

"Why don't we include the Royal Family and the Prime Minister as well?" said Alan, who for once was not his cheerful self and spoke with venom in his voice.

"Who pulled your chain?"

"I just can't believe you're being serious about this. I mean these people are top drawer and here we are talking about them committing murder and gods knows what else against young boys. I just don't believe it."

"Not what you joined up to do eh son?" said an officer.

"Leave it out," said Norman. "It leaves a nasty taste in the mouth, doesn't it Alan, but believe me old son, it's true."

"We're going to have to move fast on this," said Malcolm, trying to focus the team's minds on the matter in hand.

It was then he realised that someone was missing. "Where the hell is Claire?"

"She went out about an hour ago, sir. She didn't say where."

"Bugger it! just when I need her. Norman, ring Don Yapley and ask him to ring me here tomorrow about eleven. Don't forget to be discreet, we don't want his wife giving him a hard time. We need to know a lot more about Chief Constable Maurice Flower."

Norman disappeared into the small office while Malcolm continued issuing instructions.

"Alan, I want all the photographs in this album copied. Get onto the lab and find out when they can do it. I want them to concentrate on these group shots." He pointed to the album. "I want all the people in this book identified. I would like them by tomorrow if poss."

Alan swung round in his chair, picked up the phone on the desk behind him and started dialling.

"Right, who's got an overnight bag with them?"

Two officers raised their hands. Malcolm was pleased that they were both mature officers, because what he had in mind for them would need all their experience and guile.

"Right both of you, get up to Norfolk. I want to know exactly where Sir Henry's family seat is, and I'm talking about his house not his arse. I want to know all the gossip. How many visitors he has, who they are, is he liked – you know the sort of thing." The two men got up and walked towards the door. "And keep me fully informed."

Malcolm's mind returned to the meeting with the teachers and Claire's absence.

"I hope Claire's got everything ready for tonight. There's a lot riding on this. Where the bloody hell is she?" Malcolm was becoming more and more annoyed at her absence.

"What do these teachers actually think they're going to do at this meeting?" enquired Alan.

"They're in for a big surprise, I know that. They all think this is about cuts to their education budget. All we need is a positive ident and we can start pinning a few of these bastards' arses to the wall before they nail mine."

"You're going to have a hard job nailing anyone's

arse to the wall now guv."

Norman was standing in the doorway. Everybody stopped what they were doing and waited.

"Don Yapley died this morning of a heart attack. His wife was deeply pissed off at the news, because she's had to cancel her holiday."

"The evil bitch."

"After she had finished blaming us for her husband's demise, she handed me over to guess who?"

"Don't sod about, who?"

"The Chief Constable, that's who. Once he'd got over telling me that we're all going to be civilians, he demanded to know why he hadn't been informed of this operation."

"What did you tell him?"

"I told him to fuck off and put the phone down. It'll be all right though, I told him I was you."

"How the bloody hell did they find out so quickly? They must have followed him. What did you really tell him?"

"I told him I had a wrong number and put the phone down."

"Poor old Don. Well it's no longer a secret any more. Every bugger knows about us and it's my guess that it won't be long before they try and close us down."

"What are we going to do guv, if they try that?"

"Apart from barricading ourselves, in there's not a

lot we can do. No, we'll just have to continue as normal."

"We all know what we're doing over the next couple of days so there's no real need to come into the office at all. Hopefully, if we get a result tonight, we can open up the vault tomorrow morning and start talking to the boys in the photographs, they'll have a bloody hard job covering all that up."

"What about the office guv? Do you still want it covered at night?"

"I'm afraid so. It might be no longer a secret, but I'm not giving them an open invitation."

Several officers were already tidying their desks in preparation for the meeting with the teachers, when Malcolm noticed Alan, who was putting on his coat on and making for the door, looking very downcast.

"Everything all right Alan?"

"I'm just taking these photographs up to the lab as you asked sir. They said if I got them there straight away they'll do them while I wait."

It was obvious from Alan's demeanour that everything was not all right.

"Come in the office a minute," said Malcolm. Alan followed Malcolm into the office and closed the door behind him.

"Come on, what's the problem? If this job is getting to you, you only have to say, although I'll be sorry to lose you."

"No, it's nothing like that sir."

"Well, what is it?"

Alan gathered his thoughts. "It's not what we're investigating, it's who we're investigating that bothers me. I'm sorry, but I overheard you talking the other evening about operations being closed down because they involved important people. What was it you said, public interest or something?"

"Not in the public interest. You have to remember that when we all joined the job we signed the Official Secrets Act."

"That's bollocks sir, and you know it. What's buggering little boys and even murdering them got to do with the Official Secrets Act? They use that just to protect themselves." Alan realised he was raising his voice and calmed himself. "I know I'm just a boy in the job and your right, I am naïve, but I never thought when I joined the job that I would be part of a cover up. That someone could just stop an investigation because it might embarrass the government or the church in some way. We're talking about little children here, and now you're telling me that people do get away with murder because of their position and I'm supposed to accept it. Well I can't accept it. I bloody won't accept it."

Malcolm waited until Alan had finished.

"You have to understand Alan, you will never beat

the system."

"But I don't have to go along with it."

"Listen Alan, we have a chance of getting these bastards and bringing it all out into the open. Not much of a chance, I grant you, but I need us all together on this. Do you understand?"

"I promise you, I won't rock the boat, but I'll be straight with you sir. If we don't get a result on this because we've been closed down, don't expect me to keep my mouth shut."

As Alan left the office, Norman came in. "Problems, boss?" he asked inquisitively.

"A young man with principles. A rare commodity these days."

The phone rang in the office and Malcolm answered it. "Hello Dan, everything OK?"

"Yes, I think so, only Constable Bradley popped in to see me."

"What did he want?"

"Well I got the impression he was just passing the time of day, but then he mentioned that he had seen you next door and he asked what you were doing there. I told him I had no idea. The problem is that June was here when he called and she's now got it into her head that Derek is buried in the vault."

Malcolm remained silent, but he inwardly cursed the interference of Vincent Bradley.

"Is anything wrong Malcolm? Only June is quite upset."

"Look Daniel, I've got a lot on my plate right now and I've already promised June that if and when I find her brother she will be the first to know. Now I've got to go. I've got a meeting. See you soon."

When Malcolm arrived at the hall the chairs had already been set out and the teachers were beginning to take their seats, albeit very slowly. The journey had been thankfully uneventful. Nobody asked too many awkward questions. In fact they had been very cheerful, and many of them were meeting old friends. It was only when they saw a number of strangers in the hall that they started to smell a rat.

"What is actually going on here?" asked one of the teachers. " And who are all these people?"

"Ladies and gentlemen, if you would just take your seats everything will be explained," said Claire.

"Where the bloody hell have you been?" asked Malcolm. "Do you know what's happened?"

"Yes guv, Norman has brought me up to speed and I'll speak to you later if that's OK. It's personal."

"Is everything all right? I was beginning to get worried."

"I'll tell you all about it later guv. Right now let's get this lot seated."

"They're worse than schoolchildren, this lot," said Malcolm. "Come along now ladies and gentlemen, please take your seats and we'll get started. Any talking and you'll have to stay behind afterwards."

A sarcastic round of applause was followed by more light-hearted heckling.

"That's right. You tell them, I don't get that sort of behaviour at my school."

More laughter and jeering, but eventually everybody was seated. Malcolm looked around at his team standing at the side of the hall.

"Is everyone here Alan? I didn't think you'd make it."

Alan raised his thumb to indicate they were all present, and positioned himself by the door. Malcolm nodded to the Chairman of the Education Committee to introduce him, and he stepped forward to do so.

"Ladies and gentlemen, thank you for coming here at such short notice. I know you've all been told you are here tonight to talk about cuts in our education budget. Well I'm afraid that is not the case." He paused and looked at his audience. "The ladies and gentlemen standing on either side are police officers. They are investigating the brutal murder of one of our boys, Stephen Jennings."

Some of the more militant members started to complain. "Why couldn't they come to the school instead of being dragged out here?" asked one.

"Let me finish please. I am going to pass you over to Detective Inspector Cammock, who will explain everything. Inspector Cammock."

Everyone in the hall remained seated, although some were still grumbling and muttering to each other.

"Ladies and gentlemen, I'm Detective Inspector Cammock and I am in day to day charge of the investigation into the murder of Stephen Jennings, who as you all know was found murdered the other day. In the course of our enquiries we have found several photographs of young boys, who all appear to be of school age, and that's why you're here. We desperately need to identify these boys quickly. I'll be honest with you, we don't even know if these boys live in the area, and some of them may have left school several years ago. "

"This is bloody ridiculous!" said an angry elderly man in the middle of the audience. "You've dragged us out here into the country when you could have simply visited the schools."

"If you'll let me finish I'll explain. What you're about to see is a series of photographs of young boys. I must warn you that these photographs are sexually explicit." Malcolm saw his audience start to turn uneasily in their seats. He knew that what they were about to see would be way beyond their experience and understanding.

"That's why we need your help. If you recognise any of the boys, or even think you do, please raise your hand and one of my officers will come and speak to you. Are you ready? Jack, lights please."

The lights were dimmed and the first image appeared on the screen. Immediately cries of horror and revulsion swept round the hall. Men and women covered their eyes too frightened to even look at such depravity. Some of them retched.

"Try to keep calm, everyone." Malcolm stood in front of the screen and the reflections of a naked boy seemed to dance upon his suit. "I know they're disgusting, but just remember why you're here. It's just possible that one of these poor boys is, or was, one of your students, and we want to help them as much as you will."

Malcolm moved to the side and the group of teachers calmed down.

"Now does anyone recognise this boy?" There was no reply, and no hands were raised in recognition. Malcolm waved to Jack to continue the slides. There were more cries of anguish and indignation as his captive audience were forced to watch the celluloid acts of buggery and oral sex inflicted on the young boys by men whose faces were carefully hidden. The next slide and then the next were shown, and still nobody raised a hand or indicated their knowledge of the boys. The audience had become silent, their eyes transfixed on the screen. It was as though they had become traumatised by what they were witnessing. Many of them were openly sobbing.

God, what have I done, thought Malcolm. Had he put these poor bastards through all this for nothing?

Suddenly there was a cry from near the centre of the audience. It was the same elderly man who a few moments earlier had protested so angrily at having been brought there on false pretences.

"Do you know this boy? Sir, do you know this boy?" Malcolm called to the man, who seemed unable to speak but just nodded. Although Malcolm felt a strange sense of relief, even elation, he didn't show it. Instead he indicated to Norman to look after the man. The slides continued, and then a young man sitting at the back put his hand up, wiping the tears from his eyes as he did so.

One by one, five of the photographs were identified, by three different teachers. The lights were on now, and teachers who only a short time earlier were laughing and joking were silent. Some were still in a state of shock, while others were angry at what they had seen.

"The schools are close to each other, so it's a fair bet that these boys come from the same area," said Norman. "We're just gathering all the information now. You never know, they might even know each other."

"Take the three teachers to their schools and get the boys' addresses and any other information they have on the family," said Malcolm.

Norman was about to go. "Hold on a minute Norman. Claire, get hold of the DI of the child protection team that covers this area and arrange to meet him at his office in one hour. If you ring me later Norman, I'll tell you where it is. Alan, cop hold of everyone's details before they leave."

Alan nodded and went about his task.

As Norman was about to leave with the three witnesses, the oldest of the trio stopped and spoke to Malcolm. His eyes were still red and puffy.

"Inspector, I want to apologise for my earlier behaviour," he said. He seemed a cultured and intelligent man. "In a few months' time I shall be retiring after twenty years as head of my school and a lifetime in teaching. I like to think I did my best for my students, but after tonight I'm not so sure."

"It wasn't your fault."

"Thank you, Inspector but I rather think it was. When I came into teaching I took on the responsibility of not only educating but also protecting those children in my care."

"You're wrong sir. You're so wrong." Malcolm turned to face the teachers gathered in front of him.

"Can I have your attention please ladies and gentlemen. Before you all go home, I would like to thank you all for your co-operation here this evening. I know it's not been easy. Some of you may think you could have stopped this from happening, but let me tell you, the people who do this sort of thing are clever, resourceful and manipulative, and sometimes violent. I want to assure you that our child protection teams, together with social services and other agencies, will now be able to help these children that you've helped to identify tonight.

"I have one last request of you before you go home. I would ask you not to talk of what you have seen here tonight. Oh, one last thing, would you give your names and the name of your school to my men on your way out, It's just so we can cross you off our list. Thank you."

Many of the teachers stepped forward to shake Malcolm's hand on their way out.

"Thank you Inspector. You can rely on our discretion."

"I hope you get the people responsible."

"I don't envy your task Inspector, but good luck."

The teachers began to file out of the hall, leaving their names and the school they represented with Alan.

Alan reflected that humans were a strange breed. They had given these people the biggest shock of their lives, and without exception they'd all said thank you.

Alan's hand was still being shaken by teachers as they left.

"Thank you officer," said a man in his early thirties.

"Thank you sir, may I have your name?"

"My name?" The man looked bewildered by the request, as though he didn't quite comprehend the question, but he quickly realised that everyone else had given their details willingly to police.

"My name – why yes of course. Compton, Gareth Compton."

"Thank you sir, and which school do you represent?"

The man hesitated again, only for a moment, but it

was enough to draw Norman's attention to him and he moved in closer.

"Which school do you represent?" Alan asked again, with a little more firmness in his voice.

"Oh I'm so sorry officer. I've been so upset by what I've seen here tonight," said the man. Norman felt sorry for him and started to turn away. "St. Michael's, Lewes."

"I think you'd better come with me sir," said Alan.

The man suddenly pushed passed Alan and made for the door, but Norman grabbed him and held him against the wall. Alan joined him and together they marched the man into a kitchen area at the rear of the hall. Malcolm saw the commotion and followed them quickly into the kitchen.

"Says his name is Gareth Compton sir, from St Michael's School in Lewes, Sussex."

"Well there's a strange thing. We didn't invite anyone from Sussex. Could you empty your pockets, please sir."

"I really must protest. You have no right."

"Search him."

Alan and Norman spreadeagled the man across a table and started going through his pockets and throwing the contents onto the table.

"Alan, go outside and make sure everyone gets home safely. Ring me on my mobile when you've done."

Alan felt a little aggrieved at being sent out, but he realised they were probably doing him a favour by not involving him in whatever was about to take place. Alan left the room and Norman released his grip on the man.

"I've done nothing wrong. I demand you let me go!"

Suddenly Norman's hand grabbed the man's lower lip and in one move twisted it and forced the man's face onto the floor.

"Why did you lie to my officer, Mr... Nicholas Walker?" Malcolm said, reading the name on one of the man's credit cards.

Norman released the man's lip and he rose slowly from the floor holding his mouth.

"I was frightened. I didn't know what this was all about. I thought I was gate crashing a party. I had no idea you were the police. You must believe me."

"I think you're lying, Mr Walker. Who are you working for, who sent you? You're not the press, so who are you?" Malcolm's voice became agitated and he suddenly backhanded the man across his face. It took the man completely by surprise and blood began to flow from his nose. Norman looked at his boss in surprise. Interrogating terrorists was one thing, but this bloke was no such thing.

Malcolm bent down, picked the man off the floor and pinned him against the wall. "Who the fuck are you working for you little shit?" he hissed. He drove his fist into the man's stomach, and he screamed and collapsed on the floor.

Claire burst in the room. "For Christ's sake guv!" she shouted. She and Norman pulled Malcolm off the man. "What the fuck do you think you're doing?"

"This bastard is lying, I know it. He's working for someone. He's keeping tabs on us, aren't you?" Malcolm rushed toward the man and was stopped by Norman.

"Get a fucking grip, guv."

Malcolm calmed himself down while Norman gave the man a handkerchief to wipe the blood from his face.

"Has everybody gone?" said Malcolm, not looking at anybody.

"They've all gone guv. What do you want done with him?" said Claire.

"I want him nicked." Malcolm was beginning to get angry again.

"What are we going to nick him for then?"

The man stood quietly wiping the blood from his face, listening as his captors discussed his future.

"Theft of credit cards. He told us his name was Compton. These say his name is Walker," said Malcolm, still angry. Get two of the lads in here. I want him kept in custody overnight for interview sometime tomorrow. Is that clear?"

Norman took the man outside and left Claire and Malcolm alone.

"You all right guv?"

"Just made a complete prick of myself, haven't I?"

"I wouldn't say that," said Claire. "I've always found pricks rather useful at times." She looked at her boss and smiled.

"I'd better ring Mr Wilkes and inform him what's going on and make sure he's got that warrant and the coroner for tomorrow morning. He's going to love getting up at six o'clock. Have we got that information from the child protection teams yet?"

"I'm working on it. I've just dug their DI out of a family party, but he's going straight to his office and we can pick up all the info he has there. He's also contacting the out of hours social services team and NSPCC to find out what info they hold on the boys."

It was after ten by the time all the team had returned and all the information on the five boys who had been identified had been collated.

"Listen up. It was good work tonight. Now all we need are some positive statements tomorrow and we could be in business. So what do we know about our five boys, Claire?"

"Well, to start with they are no longer boys. The youngest is nineteen and the oldest is twenty-three. We have their last known addresses, but of course they could have moved on. We've checked the voter's register and there's no trace. The boys did have one thing in common though, and that is that they were all on the at-risk register at various times on suspicion of being victims of sexual abuse. When they left school they all lived at the addresses given with their mothers, no fathers shown. All the boys were interviewed. None of them disclosed anything at all, but it was strongly felt at the time that the boys were lying."

"Looks like those of you doing the interviews tomorrow may have a hard time. Remember, kid gloves. These boys are victims, not suspects. It's been a long day, so let's get off home."

Malcolm was about to leave the office when his mobile phone burst into life.

"Jesus, what is it now?" He listened intently to what was being said to him on the phone. "I don't bloody believe this! That lying bastard. I knew he was bent."

"More problems, guv?" said Norman.

"I'll just add it to the list."

"Our friend Nicholas Walker, remember him?" Malcolm was fuming with rage. "When they got him to Brighton nick, he handed the custody officer a piece of paper with a telephone number on it." Malcolm was pacing up and down as he spoke. "Within five minutes of that number being rung, he was released."

"You're joking!"

"I wish I bloody was. He didn't even get his name on the sheet. He just walked out."

"He's got to be Special Branch."

"Or MI5. Someone with some clout, that's for sure."

"What happens now?"

Malcolm thought for a moment and then clamped his arm on Claire's shoulder.

"We're going to give these bastards a run for their money. I've no doubt they will try to close us down, but they've got to find us first."

"Whatever you say guv."

"I want you to deal with this end, Claire. We need those boys to talk and we don't have much time. I'm sorry to lumber you, use whoever you want, tell them to be at the office by six for a briefing and keep me fully informed on the mobile. And good luck."

"Goodnight guv. See you in the morning. Hardly worth going to bed." Claire looked at her watch. Malcolm stopped and turned to her.

"You were going to tell me what was on your mind earlier on. Do you want to talk now?"

"It's all right guv, it'll wait till morning".

Chapter 23

Malcolm was up and dressed very early the next morning. He was just closing his bedroom door behind him when he noticed the brass handle of Daniel's door turning. To his surprise June stood before him with Daniel's dressing gown draped around her shoulders.

"You will tell me right away if you find Derek, won't you?"

"I gave you my word, you'll be the first person to know, now go back to bed."

"Good luck!" Daniel called from within the bedroom.

Malcolm drank a quickly-made cup of coffee, left the cottage and made his way towards the vicarage. When he reached the gate he turned and saw June watching him from the bedroom window. She waved tentatively, and he returned the gesture and continued on his way.

Malcolm thought how lucky Daniel was to have met such a nice girl. They obviously liked each other very much, but he couldn't help comparing their apparent happiness with his own feeling of sorrow at the break-up of his marriage and the loss of his two boys.

The lane was quiet and deserted, but that tranquillity didn't last long as one by one cars and vans started arriving outside the vicarage carrying Jack Digweed and his forensic team together with all their equipment. Mr Wilkes arrived with the coroner and Norman and Alan brought the magistrate.

"I bought you my spare pair, sir" said Alan, tossing a pair of wellingtons over to Malcolm, which he gratefully accepted. Both Alan and Norman were suitably attired; they weren't going to make the same mistake as they had last time and get covered in mud. Alan had also brought with him a machete, which he was using to great effect to cut a path through the undergrowth towards the vault.

Mr Wilkes produced the warrant and showed it to the Coroner.

"Well everything seems to be in order, shall we get on with it?" said the Magistrate, who was the only one not wearing wellingtons; he had been offered a pair by Jack Digweed but had declined.

Jack and his team followed Alan along the path towards the vault, followed by everyone else. They reached the steps that led down to what had been the entrance.

"Well this is it, sir" said Malcolm with fingers crossed.

"OK Jack, do your stuff, this is your show."

Jack Digweed and his team started removing the foliage from around the vault. When it was clear they started taking measurements of the vault. The whole process was being videoed by another team member.

Jack slung a voice recorder around his neck and started his work.

"I estimate the door panel is about five inches thick and as far as I can ascertain this is the only way into the vault. I am taking samples of mortar from around the entrance and recording this as exhibit JD/1. The entrance does not appear to have been opened or tampered with in any way." Digweed continued recording samples of stonework, and all the time the process was being filmed.

"I can see no other way of entering the vault other than by drilling," he said.

"Carry on Jack, you're the expert."

What looked like a large car battery was moved into position and a handheld drill plugged into it. One of Digweed's assistants started drilling while he continued speaking into his recorder. As he did so another man collected all the pieces of masonry and put them in sacks.

The hole soon extended to ten or twelve inches across. The man stopped drilling and shone his torch into the cavity, and almost immediately stepped back. The sweetly odious smell of decay, once smelt never forgotten, burst from the vault like air from a popped balloon. It seemed to hang in the air. Most people present had dealt with death in one way or another except for the magistrate, who emptied his breakfast into the bushes. Alan held a handkerchief over his nose and mouth and willed himself not to follow his example.

Another assistant stepped forward using a much larger drill, and wearing a protective mask drenched in disinfectant. He drilled ferociously, not wanting to linger any longer than he had to. The smell became stronger as the entrance got wider.

"It's all clear now sir," said Jack, who had stopped recording just for a moment while he placed a gauze mask over his face and handed another to Malcolm.

"Right, let's get on with it" said Malcolm. He placed the mask over his face, walked down the steps to the entrance and stared into the blackness. He switched on the torch, which at once illuminated the interior.

Both men stepped into the vault, ducking their heads as they did so. Malcolm held his breath as he shone the beam of light slowly around the tomb. There lay the remains of Derek Walsh, the tattered remnants of his school blazer still visible.

Malcolm stared at the body, trying to remain professional, even dispassionate, but the sight of that young boy was too much. He felt tears streaming down his cheeks, and wiped them harshly away.

"He's just been dumped in here, hasn't he?" said Jack. "Just thrown in like so much garbage. You'd better let me take over now sir. I don't want to lose anything." They both retraced their steps back out into the open air.

"It's him. It's Derek Walsh," said Malcolm as he emerged from the vault. "He's still wearing his school blazer."

Everyone stood for a moment in silence. It was Wilkes who interrupted the mood by stepping forward to see for himself the grisly remains of Derek Walsh.

Malcolm felt agitated. He was experiencing a mixture of feelings. There was elation at having found Derek's body, and a dreadful sense of loss that such a young life should be snuffed out in such a way.

"You all right Mal?" said Norman, gripping his friend's arm.

"I suppose so. I was just thinking I'd better go and tell June I've found her brother."

"Do you want me to come with you?"

"No thanks, you look after things here. Mr Wilkes said he would deal with the coroner. When they've done, get the place sealed off and I'll see you back at the office."

Suddenly Norman whirled round. "Oh Jesus! This is all we need."

Malcolm swung round to see what Norman was looking at. It was June waiting quietly just a few yards away along the path. She was still wearing Dan's dressing gown, but her feet were bare and covered in mud. Daniel came running along the path in an attempt to catch up with her.

June started to walk towards the open vault, but Daniel gently held her arm. She seemed too dazed to resist.

"You wait here Norman, I'll deal with this," said Malcolm.

"You've found him, haven't you? You've found Derek."

"I'm sorry June, we still have to confirm it, but yes I think it's Derek."

Malcolm's words of comfort were lost on June. She quietly turned and walked slowly back along the path towards the cottage with Daniel.

Norman stood beside his friend. "You OK?" he said quietly.

Malcolm nodded, and they rejoined the others.

"How long will your boys be, Jack?" asked Wilkes.

"Several hours, at the very least."

"Right, I'll arrange for some uniformed officers to get down here and cordon off the road so you won't be disturbed. Malcolm, you and your team get back to the office and start working on those boys. We want hard evidence, so we can stuff these bastards."

Malcolm thanked everyone for their help, but before he left with Norman and Alan he took one last look at the tomb. It was already brightly illuminated so he could see quite clearly into it without going in. He wanted to remember this day and the awful sight of a young boy's body so that when well-meaning people poured scorn on the idea of reinstating the death penalty he could tell them exactly what it was about and where he stood on the issue.

As they drove past the old church tower, he saw Andrew Summers standing by the entrance to Drovers Alley, his dog lying motionless by his side. He pulled up alongside and wound down the window but before he could open his mouth, Andrew spoke.

"I know you've found Derek, I saw June and the vicar. Just don't let them get away with it." With that he turned and walked off along Drovers Alley.

When they reached the office, Claire was writing the names of the five boys on the board. Alongside the names were three columns, headed. LOCATED, STATEMENT and WITNESS.

"Any news yet?" said Malcolm, pouring himself some coffee.

"Give them a chance, they've only just started."

It was mid-morning before the first telephone call

came in from one of the interview team. Claire answered the phone, but it was clear from her sombre mood that it was not good news.

"It's Team One. They've located the boy's mum and her new partner. They'd only moved a few streets away from the address we had for him."

"Don't tell me, he doesn't want to know," said Malcolm.

"He committed suicide when he was sixteen. He hanged himself in his bedroom. Mum never understood why."

"She bloody does now," said Alan, and he threw the book he was pretending to read across the room.

No one said anything. He was best left alone. Claire wrote 'DECEASED' on the board alongside the boy's name.

It was nearly an hour before the phone rang again, and once again Claire was first to answer it. This time a smile appeared on her face. The three men stood in front of her desk, like three runners waiting for the off.

"It's the top name guv." Claire was pointing to her board. "He's now twenty, married, with a small boy of his own. He burst into tears when they told him what it was about. His wife knew nothing about it, but she's a real brick."

"Is he prepared to give us a statement?"

"Yes. He's doing it right now," Claire replied.

The phone rang again. This time Alan picked up the receiver.

"Team Three, sir" Alan relayed to Malcolm. "Yes, OK, I'll tell him." Alan was busy writing notes as he replaced the receiver.

"Come on, let's have it," said Malcolm impatiently.

"Sorry sir." Alan was still busy writing down the information.

"How long is this going to take?"

"Its bad news sir, the boy also committed suicide two years ago."

"I don't fucking believe this. Two out of the five boys are dead, for Christ's sake." It was now Malcolm's turn to express his anger, and he kicked a chair across the room in his frustration.

"That's going to be a great help." Claire's words were cutting, and they were directed straight at Malcolm. He raised his hands in silent apology.

"God, give me a good armed blagger any time. Dealing with this crap all the time would send you round the twist."

"It's just a question of waiting now guv, nothing more we can do." Norman poured some fresh coffee into the mugs and handed them around the table.

One by one the interview teams were returning to the office and informing Claire of the results of their endeavours.

"We've traced all five of our original victims," said Claire. "Two have committed suicide. Two deny any involvement at all, even after being shown their own photograph. They still denied it was them. Only one of them is prepared to make a statement and it's being done right now. I've asked them for regular updates."

The phone rang again. This time Norman answered it.

"I think you must have a wrong number. Yes, this is a police station. Leave me your number and I'll see what I can find out for you."

"What was that about?" asked Malcolm.

"I think we're in the shit," said Norman. "This guy says he's a friend of Don Yapley and he will only speak to you. He also says he's a Chief Inspector from the Manchester complaints authority."

"If he wants to stick me on he'll have to come down here and do it. What's his name anyway."

"Roger Haines."

"Do me a favour Norman. Check him out first and I'll call him back later."

"Leave it to me, boss." Norman disappeared into the small office and closed the door behind him.

Malcolm sat at the large table and smiled to himself.

"Well at least you're happy about something," said Claire.

The phone rang again.

"Yeah. DI speaking. Any luck?" Malcolm's face lit up and he raised his hand for everyone to be quiet. He took his pen from his breast pocket and signalled to Claire for something to write on. She immediately laid a pad of paper in front of him and Malcolm started writing. Everyone stopped what they were doing. They could see the excitement on their boss's face and knew it was important.

"You've done a great job, well done."

Malcolm replaced the receiver and held his head in his hands. Nobody said anything.

"We've got them," he said quietly.

"Come on then!" Claire, like everyone else, was impatient to know.

"That young man, you know the one that's married with a baby." Malcolm paused for a moment. "He's come across with everything – names, dates, times, places. He's even got all the car registration numbers of all those involved."

Some of the officers started to cheer at the news, but Claire quietened them with a raised hand and a scowl. This was not a time for self-congratulation. They still had work to do before these so-called men would be charged.

"Did he mention the tower, guv?" said one of the team.

"Yes. He was taken there on several occasions, but he was always on his own. There weren't any other boys there." Malcolm hesitated for a moment trying to imagine what the boy must have gone through. "He was only eleven when the abuse first started."

Nearly everybody lowered their heads and in their own minds tried to imagine what it must have been like for that young boy.

"Can he recognise anyone from the tower?"

Malcolm shook his head. "They always wore masks and dressed like monks. He was taken there by another man who used to collect them and take them to wherever."

"Those poor kids. But why didn't their parents know?"

Malcolm just looked hard at Claire, and the awful realisation dawned on her.

"You're bloody joking. You don't mean…" Claire could hardly believe what she was saying.

"His mother got paid in cash for renting him out to these bastards. She died last year. It's strange that after everything that woman did to him, he is still protecting her and is adamant that her name must never be mentioned accept as a caring, loving mother."

Malcolm passed the paper to Claire. "Get checks done on these cars and run these names through the computer straight away."

"Right boss." Claire picked up the paper and started

to read his notes.

"Is this Mulberry House, sir?" She pointed to a name scribbled on the paper.

"Yeah, that's right."

"Well you know who lives there don't you?" A broad smile swept across her face. It was now Malcolm's turn to be kept waiting.

"It's your friend and mine Sir Henry Winterbourne. The lads found it last night."

"Are they still down there?"

"What do you think? They're booked into a great little pub which has unusual licensing hours."

"Tell them to stay there until told otherwise. That won't be difficult for them."

"They'll be devastated!"

"Our witness talks about this house having a secret room where all the boys were taken. Apparently it even had an altar."

"These bastards need putting down," said one of his team.

"He also said that sometimes there would be as many as twenty men and a dozen or so boys. He's given us the names of three other boys – well they're not boys anymore, they're young men, but he's kept in touch with them. They all knew that one day the truth would come out and he reckons they'll all make statements. It's just fucking unbelievable."

"I'll get this lot sorted. Let's hope we get some corroboration from the other boys." Claire reminded Malcolm what he already knew. One man's evidence would never be enough. They needed corroboration.

Norman had been standing just outside the small office. He had heard most of what had gone on. He handed Malcolm a piece of paper.

"I'm afraid Chief Inspector Haines checks out. Apparently he's highly thought of and he gets all the griefy complaints."

"I suppose no one will argue that I qualify for that honour."

Malcolm went into the office and closed the door behind him. He sat at the desk and dialled the number in front of him.

"Is that Chief Inspector Haines?" Malcolm listened to the reply, which was not what he had expected.

"Yes it is, and before you get the wrong end of the stick, I want you to know that I was a close friend of Don Yapley. You are aware that he died?"

"Yes, I'm aware of that" Malcolm was still very cautious.

"I can certainly appreciate your reticence, Malcolm, but it is because of Don that I know what you are dealing with. I know all about his trip to London and his meeting with yourself and Norman."

"I really don't know what you're talking about, Chief Inspector. I think you must be confusing me with someone else."

"Don said you would be a disbelieving bastard. Ex-army intelligence, aren't you? Let me lay my cards on the table, Malcolm. The last thing Don said to me was that I could trust you. So listen and listen carefully. As of eight o'clock this morning, Chief Constable. Maurice Flower has been suspended from duty."

"I don't believe it. How do I know you're telling the truth?"

"Watch the lunchtime news. And about the files regarding those two boys – you know who I'm talking about, don't you?"

Malcolm kept quiet for what seemed like ages. "You mean Russell Downs and Dominic Brewer," he replied quietly.

"The Assistant Chief Constable is contacting the Home Secretary today, with regard to an outside force investigating Mr Flower and his activities. He is also appointing a senior officer and a fresh team to reinvestigate the matter of the two boys. As soon as he's been appointed, he will contact you. Hello? Are you still there?"

"Yes I'm still here. I'm sorry. Everything has moved so fast. When did Don tell you about this?"

"Don and I joined the job together. We went our

separate ways, he went into CID and I stayed in uniform. I'm the first to admit that I've spent most of my time behind a desk. Don confided in me at the time of the investigation. I was a sergeant then, but when I made inspector I was put in charge of reorganising the records branch. It was me who tagged those files for him so that if they were ever asked for I would be informed, hence when you asked for them I told Don."

"If they are really going to re-open those cases, I know a man who will be invaluable in finding that boy in the grave yard. His name is Professor Matthew Kennard. If it's OK with you I'll get my Chief Superintendent to contact him ASAP. His name is Wilkes. I hope you don't mind sir."

"Any help you can give us will be gratefully received."

Malcolm replaced the receiver and re-joined the others in the main office.

"Get me Mr Wilkes on the phone. Then get me Professor Kennard, he'll be somewhere between the earth and the moon. We've got the bastards. Now listen up!"

Malcolm relayed what he had just been told.

"They'll have a hard job shutting us down now," said Claire.

"It's too big, too many people know about it," replied Norman.

"I hope you're right. We just need a little luck."

The phones were now ringing all the time, as members of the team were ringing in and updating information. Several other names of possible victims were added to the board. Alongside their names were their personal details. The words 'statement refused' were written alongside several. Alongside another was the word 'deceased'.

"Jesus, that makes three of them that have topped themselves," said Malcolm. Then he saw the word 'statement' beside two other names.

"Do we know what they're saying yet?"

"Not yet guv. The team will let us know as soon as they have any information. They know how important it is."

As Claire spoke, an officer was talking to someone on the phone. He gave the thumbs up sign to Malcolm and Claire.

"They've just confirmed it sir. The other two victims are telling the same story. A secret room in a big house, how there were lots of men and young boys. Some of these men liked to dress up. One of them was also taken to the tower. They all talk about being picked up from home by a bloke with an accent."

"What sort of accent, do they know?"

"German sir. They all say he was German."

"That housekeeper of Daniel's, she was German. Her old man was the gravedigger and it was him who got killed in the fire at the vicarage!" Malcolm was on a high. "Have we checked out those cars yet?"

"The list is just coming out now sir," said one of the computer operators.

Malcolm scanned the list of names that were shown on the national computer as owning the cars whose number the boy had noted down all those years before.

"It's here. Schneider. He was the driver who picked up those kids. And Sir Henry's car is listed as well."

"Have you seen the rest of the names on this list?" Norman was looking over Malcolm's shoulder, scanning the list of names.

"Those two used to be MPs. One of them still is. This one, he's a barrister. I remember him. He ripped me up for arse paper at the Old Bailey. This is like a page out of Who's Who."

They studied the list of names carefully.

"What do you want to do now, guv?"

"Have we got hold of Mr Wilkes yet?"

"He's on his way."

"Right, until he gets here, I want all these names checked out. I want to know if they're still alive and where they're living now, but let's do it discreetly."

The team set about collating and updating the information, while the computer operators were working flat out feeding in all the information. Another board had been set up, containing the names of suspects together with the index numbers of their cars and any other relevant information. A file was created on each suspect. It contained every scrap of information that might prove useful later on in the investigation.

Chief Superintendent Wilkes arrived at the office direct from the post mortem. Malcolm Claire and Norman followed him into the small office.

"They can't say at this stage how Derek died, but they have found traces of a drug. It's as yet undetermined, but they're doing a match with the one found in Stephen Jennings."

Malcolm then recounted the fast-moving events of the past few hours and showed him the list of names they had come up with. They then spent over an hour in conference deciding the best course of action. It was decided that Wilkes and a member of the team should go to Manchester and liaise with Chief Inspector Haines. They would introduce Professor Kennard with regard to searching the cemetery in St Andrew's church in Boothstown.

"If that boy is there, we're going to need the professor to find him," said Norman. "Any luck in locating him yet?"

"Not yet. We're leaving messages all over the country for him to contact us ASAP," replied one of the team.

"What's your next move going to be, Malcolm?" asked Wilkes.

Malcolm was deep in thought. "We'll go with what we've got sir. The sooner we start nicking a few of these bastards the less time they'll have to apply pressure, especially if we drop a few hints to the press about what we're doing and who's involved. After all, that bloke who infiltrated the teachers' meeting wasn't there for the benefit of his health. Somebody sent him."

"Do you really think they will still try and close us down? Even after what has happened in Manchester?" asked Norman.

"I did promise to keep that prick Kendrick fully informed, but what I don't know can't hurt me. After all, I'll be in Manchester when the shit hits the fan and hopefully you'll have a result by then."

Wilkes smiled broadly. "Tell whoever you're going to send to Manchester with me to pick me up at my H/A." He left the meeting and the others re-joined the rest of the team in the main office.

"OK everyone, take a seat, we're going to start nicking these perverts," Malcolm began. There was an air of exhilaration in the office as the team seated themselves around the table.

"Tomorrow morning you're going to arrest everyone on that board over there." Malcolm pointed to the list of suspects. "Claire will divide you into teams of three. Now if possible I want a co-ordinated operation, but at this short notice that might be asking too much. Now when you nick these bastards I want a thorough search done, and I do mean thorough. I know I've gone over this before, but I want you to bear in mind that a lot of these perverts like to collect and keep records of their exploits. It might be on video, photographs, computer disk. It might even be in letters they send to each other. If you're not sure, take it. And remember, some of these people are well versed in law. Jesus, some of them are the law, so do it by the book. If at all possible, I want them charged and kept in custody. I want two of you to stay with the prisoner and the third member of the team to come back here for a trip to Norfolk."

"If you're going to nick Sir Henry and search his house, it might be better to get a warrant. I know we don't need one, but it might be better, given who he is sir."

"That's a good idea. Alan, get hold of that magistrate who was with us this morning. After what he saw he'd give me a warrant to search Buck House, but don't mention the name, sort out the paperwork and we'll pick it up on the way tomorrow."

It didn't take long for Alan to contact the magistrate and as Malcolm had said, he was only too pleased to help.

"He'll be waiting at home sir. We can go whenever you like," he told Malcolm.

"Well done Alan. Listen everyone, do what has to be done and then get off home. You've got an early start tomorrow. I'll leave everything with you Claire, and remember I'm covering the office tonight, so I'll see you all bright and early."

"I need to speak to you before I go guv. It's important," said Claire.

"Sounds serious, you'd better come in the office."

She followed Malcolm into the office. "It's about the other day guv. You know, when I disappeared for a while"

"Bloody hell Claire, you don't have to worry about that."

"No, you don't understand. I went to see Alice."

Malcolm was speechless.

"And her boyfriend, he's a really nice bloke, although a little old for me. Even at my age I prefer them under seventy-five and they must have their own teeth. I can't stand men with false teeth, but I suppose I'll get used to it as I get older."

Malcolm didn't know whether to hit her or kiss her.

"What... how... I don't understand?"

"And stuttering. I don't like men who stutter."

Malcolm was now out of his seat and leaning across the desk.

"Tell me what happened."

"You know, you two want your bloody heads banging together. She's missing you just as much as you're missing her, and for your information the reason she hasn't been at home is because she has been staying with her friend Maureen, who incidentally has only just moved and is not on the phone yet, and the other reason she is staying there is because your water tank split and dropped fifty gallons of water down the stairs. Alice didn't know how to turn it off, so Bob – you remember Bob, your next-door neighbour? You know, the nice old ex-royal artillery bloke who wants to throw brandy down your throat every time you go out in the garden?"

Malcolm nodded. It was all he could to stop himself crying. It was the best news he had ever heard.

"Well Bob turned off the water and he's been going in every day drying the place out. The electric is back on now, so ring her." Claire leaned across the table and grasped Malcolm's face. "Hello? The lights are on but is anyone at home? Tell her you love her. Tell her you miss her. Talk to her." She smiled at her boss and got up. Malcolm hugged her close.

"Thank you" he whispered. "Thank you."

"Don't forget to lock the door. And talk to those boys of yours, they're lovely."

Claire closed the door behind her and Malcolm poured himself a Jameson's and reached for the phone.

Chapter 24

Malcolm was woken from his slumber by the sound of a key turning in the office door. He looked at his watch and realised that it was nearly five o'clock and the first members of his team were beginning to arrive. He had spent the night sleeping in a chair with his feet propped up on the desk, and it took a few moments for the blood to start circulating around his legs.

"With respect sir, you look like shit. Do you want some coffee?"

"Well, as you said it with respect Alan, yes please."

The rest of team were gathered and Claire wasted no time in organising them into their various squads.

"OK, listen!" she called above the chatter and the

rattle of cups. "You all know what teams you're in and which of these gentlemen you're going to nick." She laid several files on the table, which were gathered up by the officers.

"Now some of you have got further to go, so you'd better get going, but before you dash off I want you to listen, and this is important. When you've nicked your man and searched his drum, let me know straight away. I will then tell you which nick to take your prisoner to. I don't want you all turning up at the same police station and upsetting the custody officer. Do you want to add anything boss?"

"Only this, I just want to say thank you for what you've achieved so far. It's been a great team effort. And when you nick these blokes, don't mention Sir Henry or anything to do with this investigation. Good luck."

The team broke up, each team wishing the others good fortune. Malcolm and Claire watched as they left the office, then Claire locked the door behind them. As she did so she turned to Malcolm, who was pouring out two cups of coffee.

"Do you always look that first thing in the morning? You look like shit."

Malcolm laughed and handed her a cup of coffee. "You're the second person to tell me that, so it must be true, but at least Alan said it with respect," Malcolm joked.

"Well he would, he's not about to retire like me. Anyway how'd you get on last night? You did phone her?" said Claire, changing the subject.

"She's going to come to the cottage tonight. I told her I might be late, but she said she didn't care." Malcolm had a boyish grin on his face. He felt like death and his body was still aching from sleeping in the chair, but he was happy.

"I'm really glad for you, she's a nice lady. Now all we can do is wait. Why don't you go and have a wash?"

The first call came into the office just before seven o'clock. Claire answered the phone and began making notes. She then replaced the receiver.

"One down, eight to go."

"Did they find anything?" asked Malcolm.

Claire smiled, her smug smile.

"Come on, what did they find?"

"Photographs of some of our boys, several videos of child porn and a diary full of names and addresses."

"Yes!"

"You know this is going to take some time. Why don't you go back to the cottage and have a shit, a shave and a shampoo, get yourself cleaned up, you won't get another chance before tonight. So long as you're back here by eleven."

"You always did have a way with words."

Malcolm finished his coffee and made for the door. He turned to say something, but Claire was ahead of him.

"Yes, I'll keep you informed of any developments. Just be back by eleven."

It was only a short drive back to the cottage, but it gave Malcolm time to collect his thoughts. So much had happened, and so quickly. It was hard to take it all in. He was trying to understand the complexity of the investigation. Even in Army Intelligence, it had never got this complicated. Did Mrs Schneider know what her husband was doing? She must have done. What did Dan call her? His right hand. Well, they were never going to find the answer to that one. He had always thought he knew who the enemy was before, but now he wasn't so sure any more. The picture of young Derek Walsh lying in that tomb came into his mind. He shook his head, trying to rid himself of the memory, but he knew it would never fade. Perhaps he never wanted it to.

He parked his car alongside Dan's Hillman and went inside the cottage. He heard voices in the kitchen and went through to join them, but was surprised when a large Airedale dog padded towards him wagging its tail.

"Hello Andrew. I didn't expect to find you here."

"After what happened yesterday at the vicarage I thought I would come round to offer June some support."

"That's nice of you. How are you, June? I'm sorry it was such a shock for you."

"At least now I can give Derek a decent burial. Will you ever find his killer?"

"I don't know but what I can tell you is that even as we speak my men are arresting some very important people."

"That's wonderful. Is Derek's murderer amongst them?" asked Dan.

"I honestly don't know. We won't know until we've interviewed them, and even then it's unlikely." Malcolm stifled a yawn.

"Oh. I'm sorry Malcolm. You've been up all night and here we are giving you the third degree. Go and get cleaned up and then have some breakfast with us.

"That's the best offer I've had. No, that's not true Daniel, I hope you don't mind, but I rang Alice last night and she's coming here tonight. You don't mind if she stays, do you? I've warned her I'll probably be late."

"Of course not. I'm delighted," said Dan.

"That's wonderful news. I'm so glad you're getting back together" said June. She realised as soon as she had opened her mouth that she wasn't supposed to know, but she smiled anyway, and Malcolm didn't mind.

Malcolm took the stairs two at a time. He felt a peculiar thrill, like a schoolboy on his first date. "Just don't act like one," he told himself. A few minutes later he stepped out of the shower and wrapped a towel round his waist. He stood in front of the mirror, flexing his muscles and holding in his stomach.

"God, you're out of shape," he muttered to his reflection. He allowed his stomach to bulge over the towel, finding its natural level. Then he spread shaving soap over his stubble and shaved. When he had rinsed off the residue, he looked back at his reflection in the mirror. "You've got a second chance with Alice. Don't waste it."

He changed into clean clothes and felt refreshed and confident as he straightened his tie. For the first time in a long time, he was thinking of something other than the bloody job. He had missed Alice more than he had ever imagined he would, and he wasn't going to let this chance slip by.

He went downstairs and into the kitchen. The smell of a fried breakfast was mouth-watering. Daniel and Andrew were already tucking into theirs.

"Sit down, it's all ready for you," said June, sliding the eggs onto his plate.

"You'd make someone a lovely wife," said Malcolm, holding his utensils to attention in readiness.

"I hope so."

He was only halfway through his breakfast when his mobile phone went off.

"Here we go again," he said as he laid his cutlery

down. "Still, mustn't complain. I wonder how many bodies are in the bin now." His feeling of excitement vanished when he heard Claire whispering down the phone.

"I can't hear you," he said.

"I'm in the loo, that's why. Don't say anything, just listen."

"Are you all right?"

"Please guv, just shut up and listen. They're closing us down!"

"Who are for Christ's sake? Claire, talk sense."

"I've got two blokes here from the Crown Prosecution Service and a Commander from the Yard."

"They can't close us down, it's gone too far."

"Well, you tell them that."

"Oh shit, let me think!" Malcolm's brain was turning somersaults. "Do they know about the arrests?"

"Yes, they know everything. It was all on the board for them."

"Where do they think I am?"

"On one of the raids."

"What about Mr Wilkes, where do they think he is?"

"Playing golf, would you believe, but they're going to ring his wife. She's bound to tell them."

"I'll deal with her. What pub are George and Frank staying at in Norfolk?"

"The Crown, just outside the village of Gayton. I've got to go."

Malcolm could hear someone banging on a door and calling out her name before the phone went dead.

"What do you mean, closing you down? Who's closing you down?" June was outraged. Malcolm tried to ignore her. He was trying to formulate things in his mind.

"Listen if you want to help, just do as I ask," he said. His voice was forceful and resolute. This was not a time for discussion.

"Get me the number of the Crown, near Gayton in Norfolk."

Daniel went through to the hall and started dialling. Malcolm rang Mrs Wilkes and explained what had happened. "Don't worry, I'll phone him and let him know," she said. Mrs Wilkes was always so calm, just like her old man.

Malcolm managed to get hold of Alan and Norman before they returned to the office and gave them new instructions. Daniel managed to get through to the Crown pub and Malcolm spoke to his officers.

"Park up near Sir Henry's house. I want to know who goes in or out. We'll be there as soon as we can."

"My god, is Sir Henry Winterbourne involved in all this as well?" said Andrew. "No wonder they're trying to close you down."

"Is he one of those responsible for my brother's

murder? He was the Home Secretary for god's sake." June was becoming very angry, and no one could blame her. Daniel put his arm around her shoulder, but she shrugged it off.

"I won't stop! You know that, Malcolm. I don't care what they do. I won't stop until my brother's murderer is locked up, or better still, strung up!"

"This goes far beyond just politicians," replied Malcolm. These people are from the cream of the establishment, and they've been covering each other's backs for years. That's why they've got away with it for so long."

"What do you intend to do now?" asked Dan.

"I intend to search Sir Henry's house, and if he's there I'll nick him."

"Is there anything we can do?"

"Look after Alice when she arrives and relay any calls to my mobile."

They all followed Malcolm out to his car.

"I'll make sure Alice is comfortable," said June.

"Will you tell her something from me?"

"Of course. What is it?"

Malcolm felt a little awkward. "Just that I love her."

"Don't be daft. You can tell her yourself." But Malcolm didn't hear her reply; he was already off down the drive.

After picking up the warrant from the home of the magistrate, the journey to Norfolk was uneventful, but Malcolm was constantly looking in his rear-view mirror to see if he was being followed, and he made several detours to be on the safe side. As he approached the village of Gayton, he passed the stately home of Sir Henry Winterbourne. It was a large, imposing house set well back and fronted by a row of tall fir trees that almost shielded it from the road.

He saw the unmarked police car some distance from the house, tucked in beside some trees. As he drove towards it, the vehicle flashed its lights and Malcolm drew alongside.

"Anything happening?"

"Nothing at all guv. There's been no movement at all. Only the gardener, and he's there now. Norman and Alan are waiting for you in the pub down the road. You can't miss it."

"Wait here. I'll be back shortly."

As he entered the pub, most of the regulars turned to look at him. Malcolm saw Norman at the bar and walked across to him.

"Hello boss, Alan's sitting over there. I'll bring your drink over." Norman indicated a table near a window.

"Do both of you know what's happening?"

"All I know is they're trying to shut us down sir."

"There's no 'trying' about it, Alan. They have shut us

down." Norman had joined them at the table and placed a pint in front of Malcolm.

"You both better understand that as far as I'm concerned, you two know nothing about this operation being closed down," said Malcolm. "When the wheel comes off, which it's going to, I'll take full responsibility."

"Can I just ask" said Alan, "only we are here to nick Sir Henry, aren't we?"

"Shhh, keep your voice down. You don't think I've come all this way to photograph his house do you?"

"Excuse me," said a voice behind them. All eyes turned towards the landlord, who was standing behind the bar and eyeing them with interest.

"Is one of you Detective Inspector Cammock?"

"I should have worn a placard around my neck," muttered Malcolm to his men. "Yes sir, I am."

"Only I've got a message for you from a Mr Wilkes. I hope I've got this right – he says the Professor has found another one, and can you ring him on this number."

The landlord handed a piece of paper to Malcolm, who thanked him. Malcolm went outside to make his phone call. He came back a few moments later and sat down.

"They've found Dominic Brewer," he whispered. "And that's not all. Maurice Flowers topped himself this morning."

"Bloody hell! Well I suppose that's half a result, but where does that leave us?"

"Let's go and see what Sir Henry has to offer."

The trio rose as one from the table and left the pub, watched by the landlord. They drove straight to the property, through the gates and up the long, sweeping driveway to the magnificent house. George and Frank followed them in and parked at the side. The front door was guarded on both sides by two stone pillars, and above the door was a shield that bore the family coat of arms.

"The house is empty. What do you want?"

They turned to face the man who had spoken with such conviction.

"Who are you," said Malcolm.

"That's no business of yours. Now get off this property or I'll call the police."

"Save yourself the time, we're already here," said Malcolm. He showed the man his identification.

"I'm only the gardener. I can't let you in."

"I don't need your permission. I have a warrant to search this place. Now do you have a key, or do I have to kick the door in?"

The old man shoved his hands deep into his pockets, as though he might be hiding something. "There's a door open round the side that's open," he said reluctantly.

"Thank you. Right Alan, you stay here with him. The rest come with me. If he gives you any trouble, cuff him."

Alan was not pleased at having to babysit an old man while the rest searched the house. He considered handcuffing the old man to the bumper of his car and joining the others, but thought better of it.

The rest of the team made their way around the side of the house, through a small walled kitchen garden, through the kitchen and on into the main entrance hall.

"According to the boys' statement, this secret room is behind the main staircase" said Norman, reading from his notebook. You get to it via a cupboard under the stairs."

"Well let's see, shall we."

At the rear of the staircase was a cupboard which looked like most other under-stair storage cupboards, but bigger. Norman peered inside the cupboard. Apart from an old wooden tea trolley and some boxes, it was empty.

"It's got to be in here somewhere," said Malcolm, with more than a touch of frustration in his voice.

"They couldn't have made it up, could they?"

It was only when Norman brushed against one of the many coats that were hanging on the wall that he felt something. He moved the coats aside. Even in the half-light he could clearly see a door handle.

"I've found it boss! Or at least, I think I have." He

twisted the handle and it moved slightly. It was then that he realised that the door had been wallpapered over to match the rest of the interior.

"They've gone to a lot of trouble to hide this, haven't they?"

He took his penknife out and ran it around the door frame, then twisted the handle again. This time the door opened.

"Have you got a torch?"

Malcolm passed Norman a torch and watched him disappear into a dark.

"Are you all right?" Malcolm asked quietly, but Norman didn't answer.

"Norman, are you all right?"

"In here boss, in here." Normans voice sounded strangely distant, and Malcolm could hardly hear him. As he entered the gloom Norman was standing only a few feet in front of him, the torch dangling limply from his fingers. From the pool of light that surrounded his colleague, Malcolm could just make out a large table.

He felt around the sides of the door for a light switch and found it. The room was now bathed in a soft light, and the table was clearly visible. It was a large oval dining table, complete with ten high-backed chairs. It was decked with finest china and glass ware and the cutlery was silver. The room seemed to shimmer with sheer opulence. The floor was covered in a thick deep red carpet. On one side of this grand room were several leather sofas and chairs arranged around a large television screen which was suspended from the ceiling. The walls were adorned with pictures and photographs.

"Jesus Christ!"

Malcolm turned to see what had upset Norman. He was standing in front of a white marble altar. It was draped with purple and gold-edged cloth, and at its centre stood a large ornate gold cross. On each side of the altar stood a brass candlestick which must have been all of six feet high.

Malcolm pulled back a curtain to find a clothes rail full of costumes and uniforms of every imaginable type. "Good god, look at this!" he gasped. On one of the walls was a collage of photographs depicting naked boys engaged in various acts of sexual depravity with men. In contrast to the other photographs the investigating team had in their possession, there was no attempt by the men to hide their faces. Quite the contrary – these men openly revelled in their enjoyment.

"Those poor kids! How did they ever survive?"

"Some of them didn't, boss." Norman spoke quietly, almost reverentially. "Have you looked at all these photographs? There are some very interesting people here. Shit! That's the MP, what's his name, you know the one that's always banging on about bringing back the death penalty. Well, he can be the first fucking candidate."

"This is gross!" Malcolm was holding a photograph in his hand. It showed the very same dining table that they were standing beside. Around it nine men were seated with one chair empty, presumably that of the man who was taking the photograph. It clearly showed Sir Henry and his guests dressed in various costumes and being waited on by five naked boys. The two men nearest the camera were cuddling and kissing one of them. The pretence of enjoyment was clearly etched on the boy's face.

"This is some sort of club, some private dinner party for perverts. They're pretty damn sure they'll never be caught. None of them have bothered to hide their faces." Malcolm slipped the photograph in his pocket and looked at the table again. On each dinner plate was a white and gold edged card, and printed in gold lettering was the name of the guest.

"Here's your MP again." Malcolm held up the place setting card with his name on it. I'm going to enjoy nicking him."

He remembered that the other two officers, George and Frank, were still outside and called for them to come in.

"I would prefer it if you came out here Inspector."

Malcolm and Norman swung round to see framed in

the doorway a uniformed police officer. He couldn't see the insignia on his shoulder but the gold braid on the hat he was holding told him it was someone of rank.

"I do have a warrant to search this place," said Malcolm.

"I don't care what you've got inspector, come out here now and leave those name tags on the table."

Malcolm threw the tags across the table and in doing so knocked a glass against the high back chair and shattered it. He stormed outside, followed by Norman. He stopped in the main hall and was shocked to see a dozen men all dressed in civilian clothing. There was no sign of his officers.

"Who the fuck are you, and where are my men?" Malcolm shouted defiantly into the face of the only uniformed officer present, who he could now see held the rank of commander. He studied the men who surrounded him, and recognised the type. These men weren't police or Special Branch or even MI5; they were enforcers. They cleared up the mess left by others, and they were good at it.

"I am Commander Forbes. Your men are outside and probably on their way home by now. As for these gentlemen, they are no concern of yours." Forbes spoke in a quiet, cultured and condescending manner. "You should have done as you were told, Inspector."

"What do you mean?" said Malcolm angrily.

"You were told to curtail your investigation and you didn't. You took it upon yourself to conduct your own maverick enquiry. That is why I am taking over your investigation."

"You mean close it down! Cover it up! Do you know what these bastards have done?" Malcolm pointed back towards the secret room. Have you any idea what went on in there?"

"Frankly Inspector, I don't care. It is of no concern of mine or yours."

"How are you going to stop the press getting hold of this?" Malcolm snarled. "What are you going to do, slap a 'D' Notice on them?"

Commander Forbes smiled at Malcolm. "Don't be so naïve, inspector. If you're referring to Miss Walsh and her clerical friend, they won't present a problem. She is far too neurotic, and he is just a has-been army chaplain who sleeps around. They deserve each other."

Malcolm could not contain himself any longer. His right fist came crashing down into the Commander's face, sending him crashing to the floor. Almost instantly a man standing close by produced a small metal cosh from his sleeve and brought it down heavily on Malcolm's skull.

Norman rushed forward.

"I wouldn't do that if I were you, Norman," said Forbes, rising to his feet and wiping the blood from his mouth. "You at least might just keep your pension."

The other men moved in closer, but Norman stood his ground. He took out his car keys and held them in his clenched fist, the metal parts of the keys facing out like knives.

"You've got terrible man management technique, you little shit. I'll maim at least one of you fuckers," he hissed. He helped Malcolm to struggle to his feet.

"Don't be stupid. Just pick him up and get out." Forbes was still wiping the blood from his face.

"You've forgotten one thing, you cocky little bastard," said Malcolm.

"Go on Inspector, surprise me."

"What about the men my team arrested this morning? What are you going to do with them? How are you going to shut them up?"

"Oh, that's already been taken care of. You don't have to worry your pretty little head about that. Run along and have a nice cosy reunion with your wife – Alice, isn't it?"

"You've been bugging the phones all along haven't you, you creepy little bastard?"

Malcolm remembered the long conversation he had with his wife the previous evening and the things they had said, personal things. "You've been protecting Winterbourne right from the start. A paedophile for a Home Secretary. Why didn't you just shoot him? It would have been a lot easier. Or is he just too powerful for any government?"

"That's not right, Inspector," said a new voice. Malcolm turned to see Nicholas Walker standing in the doorway, the man who had infiltrated the meeting with the teachers.

"I was wondering when you'd crawl in," said Malcolm. "So which government rock do you live under?"

"That's beside the point, Inspector. The point is that you were told to stop this investigation this morning and you didn't. We've let you have your bit of fun."

"These bastards have been murdering and abusing children for years. A bit of fun, you call it?" Malcolm glared directly at Nicholas Walker.

"A poor choice of words, I apologise. None the less I am not protecting Sir Henry, or anyone else for that matter. I am doing my job. I don't care about them or their cronies, and you're quite right, what they have done is repugnant, but we can't let this damaging information get out because it would probably bring the Government down, whatever party machine was in power. It nearly happened in Belgium, but it's not going to happen here."

Malcolm placed a hand on his head and felt the blood oozing through his fingers. He felt exhausted and numb.

"You've known about his activities all the time, haven't you? You've just stood by and let him and his high-powered friends do whatever they wanted. Even murdering little boys."

"Let me assure you Inspector, Sir Henry had nothing to do with that poor boy's death, and we had no knowledge of it."

Malcolm sensed a weakness, a slight hesitation, and seized the moment.

"Sir Henry might have been upstairs taking fares at the time, but his brother wasn't, was he? He was back in his old church killing Stephen Jennings, and he wasn't alone, just like when he killed Derek Walsh."

Malcolm could see by Walker's reaction that he had hit on the truth.

"I'm right, aren't I? Sir Henry's brother is alive and kicking and murdering children. There's a nice family in Surbiton who are hoping their son is going to come home one day. Can I tell them he's dead and buried in place of that bastard's brother?"

"It wouldn't achieve anything. It would only distress them."

"How many boys is Sir Henry's brother allowed to abuse and murder before someone decides to stop him? He's murdered four already!"

Walker was visibly shocked. "Four boys? What are you talking about?"

"I presume you knew about Derek Walsh? He was the boy I removed from the vault yesterday."

"I know about that poor boy, yes, tragic." Walker regained his composure. "We did not know that he had returned to the country. Nor did Sir Henry."

"So his brother is alive? Well what about the boy they've just found this morning? His name is Dominic Brewer, and just like Derek, he was dumped in someone else's grave." It was Malcolm's turn to regain his composure, and the venom in his voice subsided. "Sir Henry's brother is responsible for the murders of four boys, two in Boothstown near Manchester and two in Surrey, and you so-called gentlemen just let him carry on. Oh, one other thing you might not know. Sir Henry's friend the Chief Constable."

"I know he was suspended, for financial irregularities."

"Suspended is right. He hanged himself this morning. It seems my spies are better than yours."

"Thank you for that information, Inspector."

"You can't cover all this up. You can't keep everyone quiet. Someone will talk. What am I saying – *I'll* bloody talk!"

"What do you think that will achieve? I'll tell you – absolutely nothing. In a few weeks' time all this will be forgotten."

"It can't be done. There are too many decent people involved. You can't silence them all."

"You still don't understand Inspector, do you? Nobody cares."

Malcolm felt his body stiffen as his anger returned. The men in grey moved closer again.

"Please Inspector, I don't wish to sound rude." Walker waved the men away and paused, choosing his words very carefully. "We are both professionals. If it were for the greater good, um, if the interests of the public were to be served..."

"I was wondering when you were going to get round to that old chestnut. It's not in the public interest – is that what you're trying to tell me? Well forget it! The public do have a right to know exactly what sort of people are making decisions that could affect their lives and who's sitting in judgement on them."

"I think you're being over dramatic and naïve, Inspector. Now, I'm afraid this discussion is closed."

Walker stepped aside and ushered Malcolm and Norman towards the front door, which was opened by one of his men. Outside he could see his car with Alan seated in the driving seat. Malcolm realised it was pointless to continue arguing with the man, and he was in no position to put up a fight. He walked quickly out of the front door and down the steps to his car, followed by Norman. He bent down at the driver's window to speak to Alan. As he did so, Alan turned a blood-stained face towards him.

"I'm sorry sir," he said through swollen lips. "I tried to stop them."

Malcolm laid his hand on Alan's arm. "It's all right Alan, you sit in the back. I'll drive." He and Norman helped Alan into the back seat and then climbed in the front.

Malcolm sat in the driver's seat looking back at Nicholas Walker, who stood alone on the bottom step, having ordered his men inside. They stood staring at each other for a few moments, then Malcolm slowly steered the car out of the grounds. Walker watched until the car disappeared from view.

Chapter 25

When they arrived back from Norfolk, the office door was open. Malcolm tentatively pushed it back, not knowing what might be waiting there for him.

The entire main office was empty. Every piece of furniture had been removed. Computers, tables, chairs even the phones had been disconnected and removed. The screens from the windows had also been taken down and the boards that once held the photographs of the child victims had gone, together with all the information about the suspects.

The three men stood in the middle of the large, empty space in silence. Claire emerged from the small office. She stood holding her calendar, the same calendar on which she had religiously crossed off each day that had brought her closer to retirement.

"They've taken everything," she said quietly." There's nothing left. They've sent everyone back to their stations. It's as though we didn't exist." She tore the calendar in half and threw it to the floor. "I might as well retire now. I'm too old for this shit."

She hugged Malcolm, and kissed him lightly on the cheek. "You look after Alice and the kids. They're the only important ones now."

She kissed Norman on the cheek and he held her in his arms and hugged her. She looked at Alan's face and saw the result of the battering he had taken. She gripped his arm gently.

"It's not worth it, Alan. Find something else to do with your life." She walked slowly out of the room without looking back.

"You'd better take Alan to the hospital and get him looked at," said Malcolm.

"What about you, what are you going to do?" Norman replied.

"I'm going to fulfil a promise I made, and then I'm going to pick up Alice and the kids and like Claire said, find something else to do with my life."

"Are you going to Jack it in boss? They won't sack you, they daren't."

"You and I have known each other for a long time, and I've done all the service I'm ever going to do for my country. If you two fancy a drink later, I'll see you back at the cottage in an hour."

Neither Norman nor Alan felt the need to say anything else. They watched in silence as Malcolm walked slowly from the office.

The rush hour traffic was heavy as Malcolm made his way towards Surbiton, and the slip road onto the A3 was congested because of a road-widening scheme. The road was narrowed to one lane and marker cones were placed every few feet. The workmen were still busy as Malcolm crawled past, and he was conscious of a black BMW saloon which seemed to be driving unnecessarily close behind him. Malcolm was very much aware that even now his enemies might be following him, so once he reached the street where the Neadings lived he parked around the corner from their neat Victorian house.

To his surprise, Mr Neading opened the door as he walked up the path, and he looked very far from pleased to see him. "Don't bother to come any nearer, Inspector, you're not welcome here," he said angrily.

Malcolm was stunned. "What on earth…"

"We've been warned about you. Just go away, we don't want you here!"

Malcolm rushed up to speak to him, but he turned and slammed the door. "Mr Neading, you don't understand! I know what happened to your son!" he shouted, banging on the door.

"I've already phoned the police," said a muffled voice from the other side of the door. "They're on their way."

"I'm telling you the truth damn you, don't you realise? It's Sir Henry Winterbourne and his brother!"

But he knew it was useless. The Neadings were a nice family, a trusting, religious family. They would never believe his story, and why should they? He found it hard to believe himself.

As he walked back to his car, a big black car drove slowly past him. Surely it was the BMW that had been tailgating him earlier? Or perhaps he was just being paranoid.

He climbed back into his car, and drove some way down the road and stopped by a post box. He took an envelope from his briefcase and placed the photograph he had taken from Sir Henry's house inside, then addressed it to June Walsh c/o the Surrey Argus and stuck a postage stamp on it. He walked the few yards to the post box, making sure he wasn't followed, and posted it.

As he turned onto the slip road that led to the A3, he was gratified to find that the workmen appeared to have finished for the day. Hopefully that meant he would be back at the cottage in time to meet Alice and start making plans for their future and the boys.

The giant JCB came from his nearside. The steel bucket ripped into his car with such force that it swept it up and over the edge and onto the dual carriageway thirty feet below. The tiny incendiary device fitted to the petrol tank ensured that it exploded on impact, and a ball of fire engulfed the entire car in seconds. Malcolm screamed for his wife before his life was extinguished.

It was just two weeks later that the investigation team came together again for the last time at the funeral of Inspector Malcolm Cammock, with Alice and her two boys taking their rightful place at the front of the church, followed by family members and friends and with many people from the village who had come to pay their respects. There was a guard of honour by officers dressed in number one tunics. Norman, Alan and Andrew Summers stood at the rear of the packed church, whilst June and Daniel sat just behind Malcolm's family, his arm around her shoulder. June turned, looked back at them and acknowledged them.

"Why isn't Constable Bradley here?" asked Andrew, "I thought he of all people would have shown up."

"Well I think he had had his time in the force and he decided to call it a day," said Norman quietly.

"Apparently he was well pissed off about what happened and put his papers in. It's a real shame, he was a good copper."

"I think he's got it about right," whispered Alan.

****

Several months later and over seven hundred miles away on a quiet country lane near the village of Alérac in the south west of France, an area well off the usual tourist route, eleven-year-old François was cursing his luck at having to push his brand-new bike all the way home. He knew exactly who had let his tyres down and removed the pump, and why. He would now be too late to take Michele to the pictures, which would leave his rival in love, André, free to take her.

He had noticed the black car drive past earlier. The GB plates stuck out a mile in this part of France. He was not concerned when the car drew alongside, and even though the car was dusty he could clearly see the gold lettering on the side door panel: 'JESUS SAVES'. It was obviously some English tourists needing directions. The window opened and a large middle-aged man with slicked-back dark hair smiled out at François. "Excuse moi, do you, er – parlez vous anglais, by any chance?" he said, with little attempt at a French accent.

François removed his baseball cap and smiled in

return. "My English ees not so bad," he replied.

"That's great. And you're a nice-looking young lad, aren't you?" He licked his lips and grinned, then turned to his passenger, a thin, older man. "What do you think, Brother Joseph?"

"Oh yes, Brother Vincent. A *delicious* young man."

Printed in Great Britain
by Amazon